The Royal Fables

Stories From the
Princes & Princesses
of the
Texas Children's Hospital

by

Marc Clark

Ideas & Illustrations
by the
Children & Friends of TCH

Marc Clark

Edited by Marian Grudko

ISBN: 978-0-9910345-4-3

DEDICATION

The Royal Fables is a labor of love dedicated to the children and families dealing with pediatric cancer every day. The five stories in this book are based on ideas from some of those in the Texas Children's Hospital, as are many of the drawings. It's an honor to work with them. All of the profits from the sale of this book go to the Ready or Not Foundation for brain cancer research.

The Ready or Not Foundation was started in 2006 after the founder, Barbara Canales's daughter Jackie was diagnosed with a brain tumor. She was diagnosed with stage three anaplastic astrocytoma, one of the most lethal of diseases for children. Today Jackie is in remission after going through many tough rounds of treatment. In the past 30 years, brain cancer has remained an enigma as research efforts have been poorly funded. RONF gives 100% of every dollar donated to pediatric brain cancer research. More importantly, through matching grants, they turn every dollar donated into two.

Texas Children's Cancer Center is the largest pediatric cancer center in the U.S. and each year treats more children than any other cancer center in the nation. Located at Texas Children's Hospital, which is ranked among the nation's best pediatric hospitals by *U.S.News & World Report*, the TCCC is the #1 pediatric cancer center in Texas.

CONTENTS

Introduction

It's said that every boy is a Prince, every little girl a Princess...

Some are actually born of royal birth. They are given every opportunity, afforded every luxury, trained to lead, taught courtesy, devotion and self-confidence.

Then there are those who are given nothing, who have struggled and fought, overcoming the most difficult challenges and yet somehow remain happy in the face of terrible problems, earning their right to be considered royalty so much so that their parents, teachers or any grown up lucky enough to be in their presence come to understand the true meaning of "grace".

I have been blessed to meet some of these children. I am one of those grown-ups.

They are the Princes and Princesses of Texas Children's Hospital Cancer Centers and these are the stories that come from their imaginations.

Their spirit is present in every one...

Brinly Pirtle's

The Princess
Who Loved Wildflowers

By
Marc Clark

PF

To tell a tale of Princes and Princesses, Kings and Queens, you often say it happened "Once upon a time." This story may have happened twice or more - I can't say.

So that everyone can accept what happens as possible we place the land as "Far, far away," when it could have been in a field or valley as close as your own backyard that's been covered over by centuries of wind and rain - again, I can't say.

Here's what I can say – what I know for sure:

This was not a kingdom with castles and moats. This was not a land filled with knights in armor or ladies in tapestry gowns. The people were farmers and shepherds and the like. They fed off the land and celebrated the gifts supplied by the earth. The kingdom sat at the foot of a mountain and spread out for miles throughout a fertile valley with a wide, sparkling river rambling beside it.

The animals that fed and worked for the people were plentiful. The land was rich and the plants and trees bore fruits and vegetables that graced the tables. The people's skin was a beautiful brown color, their eyes were bright and they lived a mostly happy life.

At this time, in this kingdom there was peace and life was good. (Not for everyone everyday of course - seriously, when has that ever happened?)

The King ruled because he was the best man to lead, not because he was born to it or killed the former king to take the throne. His people made him King because he deserved the job. He took a Queen, a wife, who was the most giving and loving.

Into this almost perfect time and place, the King and Queen were graced with what they believed was the most perfect gift of all: a daughter, and her name was Zari – which means golden.

From the moment she opened her eyes Princess Zari looked on the world as though it was all made for her - as if it was a toy for her to play with - and it made her laugh out loud.

They say that babies can't actually see faces or understand words: Zari would have proven them wrong because she looked directly at everyone's face and listened intently to what they said, and what she saw and heard thrilled her no end. You've never seen a baby so happy, so excited about everything the world put in front of her. She was, as far as anyone at that time had ever known, the happiest baby that had ever lived.

I can't say for sure that she was truly beautiful – don't get me wrong, she was adorable – but her beauty had just as much to do with the joy she spread to everyone she came in contact with as her actual features. For the most part people are judged on whatever the current idea of beauty is: full lips, a small nose, strong jaw line, high cheekbones or dimples. Then sometimes you can't explain why you find someone so attractive. They just… glow. That's what Zari did - she glowed.

Now you'd think that, as she became a toddler and then a little girl, her fascination and sheer happiness with the people and her surroundings would fade away, - but you'd be wrong. She kept the same love of life every day, every week, every month of every year.

That's not to say that the Princess didn't get hurt or ill or suffer in any way. She did. In fact, she may have been bruised and injured more often than most because her outlook was so sunny and positive she tended not to see things as dangerous or harmful: the flame of a candle that danced so gleefully in the dark, casting graceful shadows on the walls - it seemed impossible that it would burn her so; that something as delicately lovely as a rose would be covered in thorns that pierced her skin; that animals of every kind, so soft, so fascinating, could suddenly turn around and bite or kick her. To the Princess, these were brutal surprises.

Zari's reaction to harm was so extreme - going from complete joy to startling pain – that sometimes she would faint. She would cry so violently that she wasn't able to breathe and then she would pass out and fall to the ground. No one could do anything to help. All they could do was to hold her until her breath came back.

It was awful to watch – heartbreaking for the King and Queen. They worried, and rightly so, that their little Princess couldn't handle the harshness and difficulties of life.

For even in this peaceful, quiet land, life could be hard. Homes were modest wooden structures (where the royal family lived, the house was much larger but not fancy), always exposed to heavy rains, winds and storms, cold and heat, wild animals, poisonous insects – danger everywhere if you weren't aware of it. The Princess clearly was not.

The King and Queen weren't sure if it would be better to try to protect Zari from ever experiencing anything painful or to make sure that she faced things head on so that they wouldn't be such a shock to her. Like many parents faced with a hard lesson to teach their child, they did neither.

But then, most parents are not blessed with a daughter like Princess Zari. There are very few people like her in the world: someone who sees the best this planet has to offer and does the same with everyone they meet; someone who truly listens, who truly cares and cares for others; someone whose gift of happiness is given freely and without question. They are the closest things to angels on earth.

*****

This is as good a time as any to tell you that Princess Zari's favorite thing in the world – and you may have guessed it already from the title - was wildflowers. (Which, really, were the only flowers back then. There weren't any stores or florists or anything.)

The first time she came upon a field of flowers she was a little Princess of five or six (they didn't celebrate birthdays as we do now. They counted how many seasons you repeated, so if you were born in the Spring as Zari was, they would remember that she had seen 6 of them). It was the first time she had gone with her mother, the Queen, and the women of their tribe to the Great River to fish. All along the banks of the river were miles and miles of rolling hills, covered with wildflowers: it was like coming upon a sea of colors waving in the wind. Zari ran ahead of the women, through the flowers, with her arms spread out and her smiling face aimed toward the sun, laughing out loud. For her, it was as though she was floating in a dream: so much beauty, so much warmth. She lay down among the flowers and smiled at the sun. She was certain the sun smiled back. "Thank you," she whispered. "Thank you so much."

From then on, she found out everything she could about fishing from anyone in the village who could teach her because she knew it meant spending time near her wildflowers: walking through the fields before the women began in the mornings and simply having them around throughout the day.

She felt like that was where she belonged – where she was meant to be. She had found her place and she was happy (well, since she was always happy anyway I guess it made her happy-er).

The King, already a proud and grateful father, became even more so as he watched his daughter grow into a young woman and take her place among their people. He saw her develop into the most skilled fisherwoman in the kingdom: learning from the old women and encouraging the young.

She relished every part of it and her joyful outlook spread to the women around her every day. People would say that the Princess didn't need a net or a spear; she could charm a fish into her hands.

*****

This day, as she had done most every day for years, Princess Zari ran ahead of the women to spend time among the wildflowers, walking and smiling and celebrating the simple beauty that was her life.

This day was different…

As she leaned in to smell a bunch of violet, budding flowers she felt something move across her feet. Curious, she spread apart the leaves to see a bright green, little snake. "How beautiful," she said as she leaned in closer.

Then the snake did something totally unexpected (not to you and me, maybe, but certainly to the Princess) – it opened its little mouth and bit her on the leg.

"Ouch," the Princess said aloud, "Why would you…"

Zari never finished her thought. Something was happening in her brain that distracted her - then it moved to her body. She could feel a kind of heat starting where the snake had bitten her, quickly rising up her leg, through her stomach and chest, then throughout her entire body. Suddenly she was burning up. Her only thought was, "Perhaps if I lie down in the cool grass I'll feel better." That may have been what she thought or it could have been part of a dream because Zari couldn't tell whether she lay down in the grass or fell or fainted. Any of those things are possible. All she knew for sure was that everything went dark.

When she opened her eyes, nothing was the same. She couldn't put her finger on it right away. It was as if somebody had painted the world while she slept. She must have slept. Everything was the same and yet… not: the sky above was blue but a brighter, bluer blue; the clouds were white and fluffy but seemed puffier somehow, with a shine to them as if they'd been outlined in gold. Her Mother's face appeared. Zari saw the Queen's mouth move and yet couldn't quite make out what she was saying. Everything was moving so slowly. She thought that perhaps she wasn't quite awake yet, that she was caught between dreaming and waking. Maybe that's what was happening.

The Princess felt something near her head and turned, slowly to find out what it was. Through the stems and leaves of the flowers and blades of grass she saw the snake that had bitten her. Its quick, red tongue darted out and back and it looked as though it was smiling. Then it spoke. Which, for some reason, didn't seem strange to her. "You'll be sssssafe, Princessssss."

Zari nodded in agreement and the snake slithered away.

Then she turned to see the pained images of her mother and the women staring down at her and she smiled at the beauty of them. Her mother's mouth moved but the Princess still couldn't make out the words. Then the Queen took her in her arms and held her.

Her mother's touch was different than she'd ever felt. Princess Zari knew that her mother held her in order to give her comfort but her skin was cold and... somehow it felt like... fear. Zari could feel her mother's fear. She wanted to say something to reassure her but she wasn't confident that she could speak yet, so instead she held her mother close until the warmth returned to her skin.

That was how Princess Zari saw the events but it's not at all how the Queen and the other women witnessed them. They saw the Princess stop in the field and look down then watched as her body bolted upright, her arms shot out from her sides, frozen for a moment and then her entire body started shaking. The women cried out to Zari and ran to her. They watched as the Princess fell backward to the ground, still shaking. When they arrived Zari's body was silent, her eyes open but not seeing, her skin cold. Many feared the worst...

An Older Woman discovered the blood and bite mark on Zari's leg and knew immediately what had happened. She informed the Queen that her daughter had been bitten by a poisonous snake and she immediately sucked the poison from the wound and spit it out.

Suddenly the Princess's head jerked sharply to the side for a few moments. When her head returned to face them, her eyes blinked and began to focus on the Queen.

"My daughter. My beautiful daughter," was all that the Queen could say as she took the little Princess in her arms and held her.

Zari whispered to the Queen, "You will be safe, mother. I will see to it," and held her tight.

The Queen was confused by the words her daughter spoke but then felt an overwhelming feeling of warmth and knew immediately that everything, not just her daughter, but everything would be all right. It was a calm she'd never known before.

*****

From that day forward it was as though separated into two places: how the King, Qu_ everyone in the kingdom saw the Princess and, in turn, how Zari saw the world.

To everyone else it seemed as though there had been poison left in her body from the snake bite and that it had made her slightly crazy: she'd wander off to her field of wildflowers and lift her face to the sky, standing there for hours; she would talk to flowers, trees, animals and insects; she never simply looked at you, she would stare at you as though she could see inside of you, see your secrets; when she spoke to you she would always tell you that you'd be safe and then she'd touch you and whatever seemed to be troubling you would fade away. So, maybe she was a little crazy but it was a good crazy: it was kind and loving and giving.

Zari understood how everyone saw her. She didn't really know what it meant to be crazy though. If it meant she saw everything completely differently than everyone else, then she certainly was. If it meant that, for her, it was as though the snake had opened up a door to another world and she floated through it, happily, then she certainly was crazy.

She adored the world already but this new version of it was even lovelier. In this new painted life everything was more alive. Everything took on qualities they didn't have before: colors had feelings attached to them: she could feel the coolness of blue, the warmth of yellows, the comfort of browns, red burned hot to the touch; flowers and trees would sing to her as the wind whistled through them; every animal and insect spoke to her - not

, a voice necessarily, yet clearly the words would ,me to her.

The Princess would coax a bumblebee out of a flower and the bee would tell her how each blossom offered up its sweet nectar to her and how she would leave some behind in the next flower. In that way she helped the flowers spread and they helped her gather the sugary essence of honey. The bee would lead Zari to her hive where the Queen Bee would happily share some of the swarm's syrupy sweetness.

A mole explained why living underground was so practical: you were protected from the wind and rain and it was always cooler on hot days and warmer on cold ones.

A spider taught her new ways to sew and stitch – which she passed along to the fisherwomen to create stronger nets.

An owl taught her how to keep her eyes wide open in order to take in every single thing around her.

An ant taught her how important it was to work together, a cat taught her about balance, a salmon taught her about persistence and a nightingale about how singing released your soul into the world.

A mosquito shared with her how fleeting life can be. She would exist only for a month. Zari told her: "You should taste a bit of my blood, little mosquito. It has magic in it to show you a world of love."

"Oh, I couldn't pierce your skin, sister. I wouldn't want to hurt you," said the mosquito.

"Haven't you taught me how quickly life passes? I'm sure the pain will fade soon enough," said the Princess. "It will be my gift to you."

"My sight is poor. It may not work on me."

"You will see with this, I am sure," Zari told the mosquito.

She dipped her needle nose into the Princess's skin and sipped some of her ruby red lifeblood. And she did see wonders. Images that made her wings flutter uncontrollably.

A mosquito's vision is terrible. The world is a series of murky shadows. Imagine living your life with a dark cloth over your eyes and then having it removed on the most beautiful day of the year. If mosquitoes could yell, she would have screamed her lungs out with joy (she would have also needed lungs, which she didn't have). If mosquitoes had lips she would have kissed Zari a thousand times.

Every creature was a teacher for Princess Zari.

She didn't question that a spot of poison might still be flowing through her bloodstream. She knew that a bit of poison was a cure not an illness just as a brush with death might make you more alive. Small doses are life's pleasures – it's large amounts that create its sorrows.

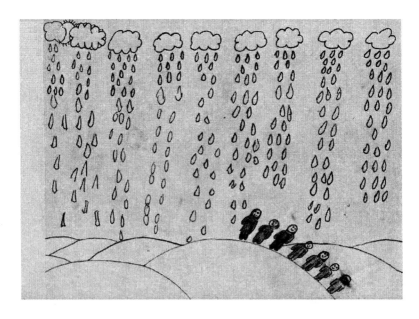

*****

One day Zari found herself in her field of wildflowers with the rain pouring down around her. She didn't mind the wet. She never did. It was the third day of constant rain; the trees drooped their arms from the weight and the wind, the river was high and furious and the sky cracked with anger. It was then that the snake slithered across the Princess's feet once more. She hadn't seen him since that day and she smiled to welcome her old friend.

"It'sssss time, Princessssss, to ssssave me now." With that, he slithered up her leg and rested in the folds of her gown.

She didn't understand at first, and then she remembered her lesson from the owl and took in everything around her… The mole and his family were out of the ground and fleeing, squirrels were scurrying, foxes slinking away, all toward higher ground. It was when a family of beavers stopped to tell her that all of their dams had burst that Zari fully understood.

She ran as fast as she could to her mother and father and told them plainly, "Please heed my words, your Majesties. We must leave. And we must leave now. Could you gather everyone in the valley at once and implore them to take only what they can carry and head for the mountain at once? Please," she urged.

You'd think that grownups, especially a King and Queen, would at least question a little girl who was telling them to leave behind everything they had in the world but they barely hesitated before ordering their men to do exactly as the Princess requested.

It was very strange but no one was afraid. No one

questioned for a moment. Princess Zari had touched each of their lives in one way or another and instilled in them a calmness and confidence that they would be safe in her care. And they were.

Thousands of people left their homes, and most of their belongings and followed the royal family out of their valley, up into the mountains. From there they watched the river explode its banks, tear across the land, wiping their homes and villages, farms and orchards from the face of the earth. For a full day they watched until the waters reached their height and finally subsided.

The following day, after the rains had stopped and the sun had found its way out from behind the clouds, Princess Zari made her way down to the edge of the newly formed lake and knelt beside it. She saw her reflection in the water. She seemed strangely older. Then she realized with a slight hint of sadness that everything around had returned to normal. Whatever gift of sight she had been given had vanished with the rains.

Something wriggled near her stomach and the snake appeared from the folds of her gown where it had taken refuge, slid down her leg and slithered away without a word.

She wasn't really sad, she was mostly grateful to have been allowed to see and hear and learn so much.

Just then a wildflower floated by and she scooped it up in her soft hands. Zari inhaled its perfumed beauty. "I'll plant you in our new home," she said to it, and smiled.

THE END

Alejandro Araque's

The Prince
Who Never Cut His Hair

By
Marc Clark

PF

Warm breezes might carry you to the island kingdom where this story takes place, though you'd have to go back in time, when only wooden ships with crisp, white sails could make the journey.

You'd travel back through centuries of time on light blue ocean waters and come ashore on sandy beaches lined with palm trees that bowed into the wind; make your way through deep green, thick forests veined with flowing streams; past sparkling waterfalls to a crystal clear lake where a castle stands, made of stone and wood, crafted with the loving hands of a people who cherished their King and Queen beyond measure.

Into this paradise was born a Prince. The moment he emerged from his mother's womb he grabbed hold of his father's finger and would not let go. The King said, "He is a warrior," so they named him Kileona, which means "strong fighter".

They didn't know how true that name would be for the young Prince.

Kileona fought against everything from the moment he could move. It was cute when he would crawl across the floor and push everything out of his way with his soft little head. It was kind of adorable as a toddler, when he would rip off his clothes and stomp around naked for all the world to see. It was slightly less endearing as the Prince turned ten and refused to bathe for weeks. (He finally did take a bath because even he couldn't stand how smelly he was. "I'll bathe when *I* decide to," he told himself, "and not when someone orders me!")

He fought against every rule just because it was a rule. Whatever he was told, he would do the opposite.

When Kileona wore rags to the great dinner instead of the royal robes he was ordered to wear, you would think the King and Queen would punish him but they didn't. They believed, as many parents do today, that this kind of behavior should not be given attention. Where a child is concerned, you praise the good and you ignore the bad.

When anyone would question the King about the actions of his son (though not many did – you're not supposed to question a King), he would say, "Some children do not learn from the good examples of their parents, some must learn on their own."

Not even when Prince Kileona refused to cut his hair. I mean, ever. During the hair cutting ceremony his people held at the start of every dry season (they didn't have calendars, just a dry season and a humid season) when the women would cut the men's hair and weave it to make strong rope, he refused.

By the time he was twelve, the Prince's hair was all the way down his back. Girls would giggle at him as he passed. Boys would sometimes mistake him for a girl. You'd think he'd get tired of it and want to cut it all off but it became a kind of badge of honor for him. He believed his hair was the thing that showed everyone he was a fighter – no matter what the cost.

As you can imagine, the one place Kileona did excel was at fighting. At twelve he was already strong, nimble, fast and confident when it came to any kind of combat. He hit his mark every time with a bow and arrow as well as a spear. At hand-to-hand combat he could beat anyone twice his age. With a knife his aim was lethal and he was aware, instinctively, how and where to do the most damage. What he loved the most, though, was fighting with a wooden staff. It was just a long, strong piece of thin wood, really, but to him it was magical – like a beautiful extension of his arms. With it, he was an artist and a warrior in one. He could spin it, toss it and strike at any place on anyone at any time. It was – he was - beauty and grace, deadly and sure.

The one person in the kingdom that Kileona didn't fight against was the man who taught him combat: the great warrior, Kanunu. He was the only man who could beat the Prince with a staff and the only person who could teach him anymore. They fought for hour after hour in every place they could find: through every room in the castle, on the beach, the muddy shore of the lake, on rocky cliffs and beneath the waterfall – any place that would pose a challenge. Nothing gave Kileona more happiness, and more confidence.

When the time came for the King to choose the young men who take The Jungle Challenge the young Prince was sure he would be the first to be picked, even though he was seasons younger than boys who were usually allowed to join.

The Jungle Challenge was a trial which every boy had to go through in order to become a man. At the beginning of every dry season, after the haircutting ceremony, the King would choose the boys he thought were ready. The great warrior, Kanunu, would take one boy at a time, two days journey into the jungle and leave him there with a just a knife. The boy would have to find his way back to the castle alone. He would have to know how to fashion weapons, hunt, fish, cook, make a shelter, protect himself from wild animals, dangerous reptiles and insects. For days the mothers of the kingdom would sing songs to the gods to protect their boy, and fathers would silently worry, hoping they had taught their boy well enough. Many boys came back from the challenge injured or sick but they would come back men. The next would be sent out, then the next and the next. Now and then one would not return and men of the kingdom would embark on the long, sad journey to find his remains. When all of the boys had completed the trial – no matter the outcome - the entire kingdom would hold a great feast and paint their bodies as men.

Kileona had dreamt of The Jungle Challenge since he was a small boy. He saw himself braving rivers, fishing and hunting, fighting wild animals and returning to the castle wearing their skins, triumphant, unharmed, cheered as a great warrior.

He stood on the great lawn with the other boys, shaking with excitement as his father entered the balcony above them, closing his eyes in anticipation of hearing his name. The first name was called. It was Makani. The Prince's heart sunk. Then he thought: "Of course. My father is wise. He would not want others to feel as though he was showing favoritism by choosing his son first." So he stood there, patiently – well, not really, but he stood there nonetheless as name after name after name was called.

Then there was silence. Silence for him anyway. The other boys were cheering their friends on, fathers, mothers, aunts, uncles and grandparents were congratulating their boys. Kileona didn't hear his name being called. Was something wrong with his ears? It was like a bad dream. He pinched himself just be sure and said, "Ow."

His dream state turned to anger and he ran into the castle, up the wide stone staircase to find his father, the King, who had betrayed him!

They met on the staircase as his father and mother were coming down to congratulate the chosen boys.

"Why was I not chosen, father?!"

"Because you are not ready, my son," the king told him calmly.

"But I am ready! I am the strongest and the best fighter," Kileona argued. "I am ready to take my place as a great warrior!"

The King remained undisturbed by his son's anger. "I have told you this time and time again: A great warrior doesn't always fight, he is wise enough to use force to his advantage."

"Yes, you've told me over and over and I still don't understand!" the Prince yelled.

"Well, when you do, you will be ready for the Challenge and not before." And with that the King and Queen left their son to join the rest of their people in celebration.

Do you know what a tantrum is? It's when someone stomps around and throws things and breaks things and kicks them and yells and screams at the top of their lungs. That's what Kileona threw, a tantrum. And it was a big one. It's kind of embarrassing to watch so everyone nearby slowly backed away and disappeared as fast as they could. It went on and on until he fell to the floor, exhausted and crying. (I know, Princes aren't supposed to cry – especially ones that want to be great warriors – but the Prince was having a really rough day.)

In time, Kileona got to his feet and dragged himself down the back staircase and out the rear of the castle so he didn't have to see and hear the huge celebration going on. He made his way to his favorite part of the lake as it emptied into the rushing river where he and Kanunu would practice their fighting. There he sat, crying and throwing stones at the water.

"Don't mourn, little King," which is what Kanunu always called him. Kileona turned to see the warrior standing above him. "You are only on the first page of the story of your life. Many things have yet to be written. Harness your anger and your sadness and mold it into strength."

The Prince tossed a large stone into the lake. "You and my father are always speaking in riddles. Why don't you just say what you mean?"

"Maybe you'd rather fight," Kanunu said throwing

Kileona his staff.

The Prince smiled, catching it and spinning it around in his hand. He was on his feet and striking before the warrior had time to grab his own staff. So he had to dive to avoid being hit. He rolled on the ground, picking up his stick in the process.

Kileona knew he had the advantage so he struck over and over and over: high, low and jabbing to the stomach and face - each time Kanunu was able to block or retreat from the blows, backing closer and closer to the edge of the lake. Knowing he couldn't keep dodging the attacks, the warrior turned and ran up a low hanging tree branch jutting out over the water. He turned just in time to block another of the Prince's jabs. Another and another and another came at him but each one was getting wilder and wilder and more and more angry.

"Don't let your anger guide you," he told the Prince.

"Stop telling me what to do!" the Prince screamed, striking again and again. Then with all of his might he swung the staff at the warrior's waist missing by just a hair and felt the staff leading him off the edge of the branch.

From his point of view the world seemed to slow to more than half its pace: he watched his staff barely miss its target and fly out into the air above the tree line; his body slowly twisting around until all he could see was the sky; falling backward through the breeze with Kanunu above him standing firmly on the branch with a small hint of a smile on his face; then the biting snap of his back as he hit the water and went under. It took a moment for him to regain his senses and when he did, he gently floated to the surface.

"Are you unharmed, little King?" Kanunu yelled down to him.

Kileona shook his head, "Yes." He couldn't find the words to speak yet. He turned his body and started swimming toward the shore, fighting the current that wanted to drag him toward the waterfall.

"Be careful of the branch," the warrior yelled down to him.

The Prince searched the surface of the water and saw a very large portion of a felled tree between him and the shore. He nodded up to Kanunu and dove under the water to avoid it.

Kanunu watched the little Prince as he went under, admiring how strong the young boy was. He watched… and waited… But the boy didn't come up. His eyes scanned the water, judging where the current might take him but saw nothing. Finally, there, near the edge of the lake as it emptied into the rushing river, Kileone's head appeared, his mouth opening, struggling for air, his long hair, caught, tangled in the fingers of the branch, one arm raised, grasping for help before tumbling over the edge of the waterfall into the raging river.

The warrior dove into the water, stretching his long, powerful arms and kicking his legs as hard and fast as he could. Knowing that the Prince had already been engulfed into the rapids he stopped himself short of the waterfall so as not be pulled into the rocks and made his way to shore. His eyes scoured the water and rocks below searching for the Prince. He saw the pieces of the large branch scattered among the rocks at the base of the waterfall but no sign of Kileona - no blood either, which was good. He knew it would take too long to make his way down the treacherous rocks and the coming darkness would make them impossible to manage. The best thing to do would be to gather a search party, so he ran for the castle.

For Kileona, his view had gone from watching the earth move slowly to everything happening faster than he could follow. He couldn't believe how quickly the large branch came toward him under the water. He was unable to dive down far enough and fast enough for his flowing hair to get clear of the clinging tentacles of the branch. His head, then his whole body was jerked backwards as the current began to pull him toward the falls. He swam as hard as he could to reach the surface and catch his breath. As he did, he briefly saw Kanunu high above him in the tree. The look on the warrior's face told him he was in grave danger.

He barely turned his head in time to see the tree branch go over the edge of the waterfall and he was yanked under after it. His scream was half out of his mouth when the water rushed in and he was taken over the falls backwards. There was nothing but falling: arms flailing, rushing water on top, down, down, down. It was like falling from a tree with someone standing on top of you and holding their hand over your nose and mouth.

Then smack! Landing full force on the branch and feeling it crack beneath him. Kileona could feel the branch rip a large gash in his side but he couldn't see the blood or the skin being torn. He was still being dragged further down into the rapids below the falls.

His hair must have been freed because the branch was nowhere to be seen and the river was taking him downstream at a tremendous pace. He managed to pull his head above the rapids for a moment and suck in some much needed air.

In spite of how confused he was, the Prince was still aware that there was another waterfall coming up soon. Any minute. He knew this part of the river well. The next falls were higher than the last and might do more than just tear his side. He knew he was lucky to have survived this far. So he turned into the rapids and fought. He swam as hard as he could: stroke after stroke against the current. He managed to grab hold of a rock with one hand but it was so slippery with moss that he lost his grip and was taken backward again.

Again he fought the rushing water and grabbed the rock - this time with both hands. But once more his fingers couldn't hold on and he was forced back into the rapids. He swam and swam and swam against the water but his arms were weakening and he was moving more downstream with every stroke. He could see the slippery rock begin to fade into the distance.

Maybe it was because his eyes were confused by the rushing water but it looked to him as though the rock began to take the shape of his father's face. It spoke to him: "A great warrior doesn't always fight, he is wise enough to use force to his advantage."

Kileona was so tired he could barely move his arms. All he could think was that he had to fight the water. He had to.

The words came back to him again: "A great warrior doesn't always fight…"

So the young Prince decided to let go. He turned his body into the rushing waters and let the rapids take him. Soon he floated to the surface and could breathe. He saw the banks of the river speeding past and the empty sky ahead as the river emptied into another waterfall.

He looked around as his body went over the falls. He could see most of the lower part of the island from here: the thick jungle; the pink sand of beaches beyond… "If I must die," he said to himself, "this is a beautiful thing to see before I close my eyes forever."

That kind of realization changes a person. Very few people are faced with death and even fewer choose to accept it when comes.

Even though he was falling a hundred feet incredibly fast, Kileona remembered a couple of things about jumping from great heights into the water (he and the other boys of the kingdom would jump from the cliffs into the lake): keep your legs straight and cover your face with your hands. Because he was so comfortable with the idea of not living through the fall he thought, "Why not give it a try?"

And you know, it's pretty much accepted that when a person is relaxed during a fall they tend to have fewer injuries.

His entrance into the pool of water below the falls was so effortless that it shocked him. The water was deep and cool, he entered it smoothly and when he uncovered his face he found it easy to swim to the surface.

Kileona's first breath above water was... It's hard to explain. Have you ever woken up from a terrible nightmare and realized, "No, I'm at home, safe, in my bed?" or fallen backward and had the breath knocked out of you – you believe you will never breathe again – and then it comes back? Well, it was like both of those things together. It was... a breath of life.

The Prince swam easily to the shore and considered his options while he applied a mixture of leaves and mud to cover the wound in his side, then lay down with his body at an angle so that his heart was below the cut. Soon the bleeding stopped.

"Surely my father and Kanunu would organize a search party to find me, - but not till morning, when you can clearly see the tracks coming from the river," the Prince thought. He instinctively reached for his long knife, tied to his belt. It was still there. "I will cut some large leaves and thick branches to make a lean-to and protect myself from the rain and wild animals..."

But he didn't. His body was so tired, he'd been

through so much that he fell asleep soon after the thought entered his mind…

*****

The morning sunlight was a new day dawning for the little Prince: the sun sneaking its way through the trees, the sound of rushing water by his head, soft sand, birds filling the empty air.

A Prince lives a sheltered life: his bed and pillows are made of feathers, shades sheltering his eyes from the glare of the sun, a gentle servant's hand warmly bringing him out of slumber.

This was so different and yet so much more… alive.

Kileona sat up too quickly and felt the tear in his side as a swift, sharp friend reminding him that life isn't always easy.

He fed himself on wild berries and then decided that

he would brave the steep rocks to the top of the falls because a search party would have to go miles around the cliffs and all the way down to the beach in order to find a safe path that would reach him. He would beat them to it and be home before midday.

Halfway up the rocks Kileona had to navigate a thin walkway to reach higher ground. As he did, the stone that he was gripping pulled free of its setting and almost fell on his head. He grabbed again and again and each time the rocks poured down at him. He was sure he would fall backward and die among the rocks fifty feet below but at the last moment one rock held and he pressed his face to it, breathing heavily and praising the gods.

As he caught his breath the rock formed the face of his father and again it said, "A great warrior doesn't always fight, he is wise enough to use force to his advantage."

"What is with these talking rocks!" Kileona said out loud. Of course he knew the stupid rock was right: fighting to make his way up the cliffs might kill him; the path around was the only way to go.

It might take a day more to go all the way to the ocean and find the path that led up to the castle but that's what he would do.

Walking through the thick underbrush of the jungle he didn't notice the sound of something tracking him. It wasn't until the Prince had taken a rest in the warm underbelly of a knotted banyan tree to change the bandage on his waist that he first heard it. It was a low grunt. The hair on the back of his neck stood up because he knew it was the sound of wild boar. Where he was sitting would allow no escape, the boar could attack and he would be trapped. The tree had no low hanging branches for him to climb...

He didn't think. He just moved. Fast. Kileona tore through the jungle, pulling his long knife out as he ran, sensing more than hearing the boar hot on his heels. His practice with Kanunu taught him to take notice of everything all around. He saw the path ahead through thick, leafy foliage, to one side the rocky cliff, to the other the riverbank, above a dying tree, behind, the pounding of the hoofs closing in. He jumped up and broke off a branch from the tree and scraped the dead twigs and leaves from it with his blade as he ran.

Now he had his strong staff and his long knife: weapons he knew, but they wouldn't be enough against a wild boar. All of that power, the razor sharp tusks.

The path ahead split: dropping off steeply and bending down toward the river in one direction, up toward the hills in the other. The boar would certainly outrun him going up hill. He took the lower path, but then a few feet down it the footing became too steep and Kileona tumbled forward. He rolled and rolled, losing his staff and ended up tangled in a sticker bush. The Prince struggled but his hair was completely caught up in the thicket, his knife in his hand, the staff a few feet from his grasp.

He turned to see the boar stop at the top of the hill where the paths split. It cocked its head slightly, taking in the situation and proceeded down the steep path, step by step, sure of its footing. The boar knew its prey was caught, cornered. It didn't have to rush.

Kileona pulled and tugged, ripping and tearing his hair by its roots. It was no good. He stopped struggling. This time he didn't need a rock with his father's face on it to hear his voice: "A great warrior doesn't always fight, he is wise enough to use force to his advantage."

He knew what he had to do. He moved at the same time the boar dug his heels in and charged straight for him.

The Prince sliced his hair off in three quick strokes of his knife and grabbed the staff. He dug one end of it into the dirt and braced it with his foot – the other end pointed toward the oncoming beast.

The stick hit the boar directly in the chest and the force took him up into the air. Kileona pulled on the staff and watched the boar sail over his head, landing in the bramble behind him. He took his knife and struck… and the beast fell silent forever.

*****

Kileona's people believed it was a sin to let any part of an animal go to waste. They would have spent hours cutting up the boar, then built a stretcher to carry it to the castle. And that's what he did.

A little way up the main path, Kanunu and a search party found him. The Prince didn't say a word, neither did the great warrior. He and his party fell in behind Kileona, taking the stretcher for him to lighten his load.

Kanunu sent a runner ahead to let the King and Queen know that their son was safe.

By the time they arrived at the castle, his parents were there to greet their son with the whole kingdom in attendance. They saw their son approaching: blood still flowing from the wound in his side; cuts and bruises across his face, arms, body and legs; the great warrior, Kanunu, not taking his place in front of the Prince or even as his equal at his side, but behind him, hauling his slaughtered prize.

Very few parents are given the gift of seeing a glimpse

of the man their son will someday be or the woman their daughter will become but the King and Queen saw it in the face of their young Prince that day. They also saw that this was no time for celebration. The Queen hugged her little boy and they helped him up to his room where his wounds were dressed and he lay in his bed and slept and slept.

The midday sun shone through his window the following day and woke him from his slumber. He gently turned his head to see his father sitting beside him.

The King reached over and took his young son's hand. "I prayed for you, my little Prince."

"I heard you father. And I understood your words... finally," Kileona told him.

"I knew you would," his father said, smiling. "The stories they are telling of you. Oh my, you will become legend."

"I don't wish that, father," the Prince said.

"Good. Then it will be deserved" the King told him, running his fingers through his boy's sheared head. "I am going to miss that beautiful hair, though."

The Prince laughed and hugged his father. "Me, too."

THE END

Brooke Hester's

The Princess
Who Was Too Demanding

By
Marc Clark

₽𝓕

Long before the people you know were born, before the books you've read were written, before the songs you've heard were sung; across oceans, into the mainland, through valleys, over mountains, beyond rivers and lakes there were the green, rolling hills of the kingdom where this story takes place.

Atop the highest hill stood the castle of this great land. Its delicate spires reached to the sky, golden and glistening in the sun. The city spread out beyond the castle like out-stretched hands, taking its heart, its mind, its soul and direction from the royal family within.

The King was a wise warrior and he chose for his wife a Queen of such beauty and grace that his heart would race every time she entered the room. They loved one another so deeply that they feared having children - thinking it might take their attention away from each other. Like many parents before and after them, they found the opposite to be true. With their first born, their hearts grew to encompass the young Prince who came forth. The same held true with each child after that. Their hearts grew and grew to love them, one and all.

The last child born to this loving, royal family was a very special Princess. Perhaps the powers-that-be saved the best for last because she possessed the strongest qualities of her parents, and it was clear the moment she took her first steps. They weren't tentative or wobbly: she put her foot down firmly and deliberately, one after the other, almost challenging everyone to get out of her way.

The King and Queen named her Lingxioa (pronounced: ling-shee-ow), or Ling for short. Which sort of means daughter of heaven or one who rules part of the sky. (It seemed as though Ling would one day rule any place she wished.)

Now, who's to say why children turn out the way they do? Some say that we are who we are from birth - that the generations before us shaped everything about us: the color of our eyes and hair and skin, the shape of our nose, hips, toes and chin, right down to our likes and dislikes, our tempers, our compassion, our intelligence, even what we remember and what we choose to forget. Others say that it's where we live and who raises us that define what kind of person we will be - that we are blank pages and everything we come in contact with helps to write the story of us: an inspiring teacher, parents who constantly fight, a good friend, a bad neighborhood, harsh criticism or a helping hand. Still others believe it's a mixture of both: you may have your father's temper and your Aunt Lei's eyebrows but one good, steadfast person filled with compassion could change you into a kinder, more caring person. So, I can't know for sure what made the Princess the way she was. All I know is that she had to have her way about everything. And she usually got it.

It's said that during the "terrible twos" (when children are two years old) kids want what they want and they want it now! Well Ling didn't appear to outgrow her twos.

At two, if she didn't want to wear a dress that her handmaiden chose for her she would cry and throw herself on the ground until she got her way. At three, she would throw the dress on the floor and stomp on it. At four she would throw it out the window. At five, she'd rip it to shreds. At six she would have the handmaiden who brought it to her removed. By the time Lingxiao was eight years old all she had to do was give the handmaiden a cold stare and the dress was never seen again.

It's also said that you can get more flies with honey than vinegar. (Which means that if you're sweet you're more likely to get what you want than if you're not nice.) It was obvious that the Princess hadn't heard that saying.

She didn't politely ask a servant to bring her fresh vegetables with her meat. She'd say, "I don't care if you have to go out and plant the seeds, water them and wait for them to grow, just get me my fresh vegetables!" You wouldn't hear her say, "Please Professor, would you perhaps consider concentrating more on subjects that might have a bit more impact on my life instead of spending so much time on battle strategies?" Oh no. It would be more like, "Forget war. Teach me something useful, you oaf!"

So, not the kindest Princess you've ever met.

You'd think that Lingxiao's parents, the King and Queen, would have recognized this unattractive trait in their daughter but they did have seven other children and a kingdom and a castle to run. Plus it wasn't always apparent.

In fact, this was only one part of Ling's personality. She had many lovely qualities. (Of course you'll hear that a lot about someone who does things that are considered not nice. People will say, "Yes, but she has a really good heart." They mean that she's an awful person but isn't terrible twenty-four hours a day.) She was actually a good person. Being demanding isn't necessarily a bad thing – it means that you fight for what you want - but when someone is *too* demanding and not so sweet about it, that is usually the only thing you remember about them.

One of the really nice things about the Princess was that she loved to dance. And when she did, she made everyone who watched forget that she had ever done anything wrong because they couldn't help but smile. She loved it so much that to her, it actually was love -- the essence of love. So when she danced she showered that gift on everyone.

Ling also loved to listen to stories. Perhaps it was because it was the one thing she got to do alone with her father. He loved to tell his little girl stories and she could listen for hours and hours about how her great, great, great, great, great, great... great grandfather banded together all of the villages and towns and established this magnificent kingdom centuries before, how a couple-less great grandfather formed trade routes with neighboring kingdoms to sell the iron ore so rich in their land and built the great palace and city surrounding it, the heroics and devastation of the ten year war with their neighbors to the north or the romantic scandal of "the dancing Princess" who chose a life in a dance troupe over a life in the palace (Ling thought she may have gotten her love of dancing from her – if that's really how it works).

What she really loved the best, though, were the stories her father told her about what the world was like before her ancestors built this kingdom, a time when deities walked the earth among the people.

The tale she always wanted to hear was the one about The Wooden Box. She would snuggle up close to the King, in her pillowed bed and ask: "Please father, tell me the story of The Wooden Box."

And he would tell her a story something like this:

*****

Before time was recorded, when the deities protected humans as their flock, this land belonged to them. The hill where this castle now stands was filled with peach trees to feed mankind, lift their spirits and give them the gift of longevity.

But the humans were weak and greedy and grew fat on the fruit until one by one the peach trees began to die out. At last one tree remained standing, with only seven peaches on its branches.

Many of the deities wanted to punish the humans for their selfishness but since they'd already lost the gift of a long life, the deity of Hope convinced them to show mercy.

She took the pits from the seven peaches and placed them in separate wooden boxes carved from the trunk of the surviving tree. Each of the pits would allow a human one wish so as to give mankind the gift of Hope.

She then scattered the boxes to the seven corners of the world – one of them being here, on this very hill, hidden from the view of the greedy , but in plain sight of the pure at heart.

To open the box, one merely had to whisper the words: "Great souls rely on their wills; weak ones have only wishes."

*****

Princess Lingxiao could not stop thinking about that wooden box. She talked about it with her father, her mother, her sisters, her brothers, her teachers, her servants and sometimes even herself (as we all sometimes do). She read everything she could get her hands on about it and even dreamt about it in her sleep.

One morning she shot up in bed coming out of another dream about the wooden box and said out loud, "I'm going to find it."

After all, what's the point of being demanding if you can't demand something magical?

With the King's permission she had word sent out to

the far reaches of the land, even beyond their borders that every small box be brought to the castle for her thirteenth birthday. If the bearer's box was chosen they and their family would be allowed to live in the castle.

Of course, the King, Queen, Princes, Princesses and much of the kingdom thought that Ling was being silly but they were fascinated to see what would happen nonetheless.

They weren't disappointed. It was a parade for the Royal Family and the city to behold: merchants and craftsmen from throughout the known world held audience with the Princess to present their beautiful boxes. Some so ornately crafted and bejeweled that their beauty would make the onlooker gasp and little girls' eyes light up; wooden boxes inlaid with gold, silver, jade and rubies.

For months the Princess would invite the owners of the boxes into the throne room a hundred at a time, open each of them and silently repeat the magic phrase to waken the spirit inside, but none responded. By the time Ling's birthday arrived she had opened thousands of boxes without finding The Wooden Box of legend. Her father, the King, told her it was time to stop. She could pick the loveliest box as her birthday gift and as a reminder of how diligently she pursued her dream – which, in itself, is an accomplishment worth noting.

Instead, the Princess demanded that she be allowed to go and look at the boxes she hadn't seen yet that were still lined up outside of the castle. She thought, and reasonably so, that the box containing the wishful spirit would be the most beautifully carved box ever seen, - a box that, once glimpsed, would make you think "Surely this box must have come from heaven." She had no doubt she would pick it out if she had just one more try.

When she walked outside the castle doors her little heart sank. The line of people holding boxes for her to see stretched for miles and miles. She would never be able to see them all, not in a day, or even a week. She hated giving up – hated it. She lifted her face to heaven as a tear slipped from her eye and graced her cheek.

Just then she heard a young girl's voice. "Your Highness," it said. The Princess turned to see a beggar girl about her age, kneeling at her feet.

"Yes? Speak," Lingxiao demanded. "Do you think I have all day?"

"It is my birthday today, the same as you," the girl said. "I know it's not much, but my grandfather gave me this box today and… I know that it's too plain and ordinary for a Princess but…"

"Yes?" Ling urged her on. "What is it you're trying to say?"

"Well… I offer it to you just the same. For your birthday," the girl said, holding up a faded wooden box, too large for her hands.

Princess Ling looked at the ugly, old box, and the selfless little girl who offered it. Then stared at the line stretched out before her with thousands of people holding thousands of boxes. Her wish would never be granted now, that was a certainty. Her father did tell her to choose a box for her birthday… and she didn't want another young girl to be as disappointed as she was on this day. "It means all the more coming from a place of such kindness," Ling told the girl. "I accept your gift. Rise and tell me your name."

Tears welled up in the young girl's eyes and spilled down her cheeks, etching white lines through the dirt on her face as they fell, dropping down and staining the already ragged, wooden box.

"My name is Yi, Princess," she said.

Ling motioned for her to rise. She bowed to the beggar girl, accepting the box.

The Princess then took Yi's hand and led her through the gates, past the Guards, to the castle garden. "Let's see if we can get you cleaned up a bit. You'll want to look your best if you're going to live in the castle with me."

Yi gasped at the thought.

"Your grandfather will join you, of course. Are there others in your family?"

"Just him, your Highness" Yi replied.

The girls sat by the fountain in the shade of a tree. Ling dipped one of her embroidered handkerchiefs into the water and began to clean the dirt from her new friend's grubby face. "Hmm. There might actually be a pretty girl under here, Yi."

Yi smiled then winced as the Princess scrubbed and scrubbed, then dipped her legs and arms in the fountain to clear away most of the grime. After a time the girl was as cleaned up as she could get without a hair wash and change of clothing (hers were practically rags).

"That's better," The Princess remarked, looking over the changed beggar girl. "You are lovely, Yi. I'm quite taken with you. Now let's look at our gift." Then added, "I couldn't bring myself to actually take your birthday present away from you, so let's just share it, shall we?"

Yi nodded "yes."

"I can't seem to open it. Where does it latch?" Ling said almost to herself, struggling to pry it open.

"It's a puzzle box of some kind, my grandfather told me. He wouldn't tell me the secret."

Turning the box over and over, Ling noticed a small line, only noticeable because of the recent stains of Yi's happy tears. "Hmm," she mused. Then dipped her handkerchief into the fountain once more and dripped water all over the ugly box. Immediately dozens of criss-crossing lines appeared on the surface. Both girls gasped together and looked at each other with wide-open eyes. "It's an adventure!" the Princess exclaimed. "Come."

With that, she grabbed Yi's hand and they ran to a place within the garden walls under the shade of a beautiful tree. They lay on the soft, fresh grass, playing and laughing together, moving and sliding the different pieces of the puzzle box to try to get it open. After hours the task became frustrating and the Princess grew annoyed. She finally yelled out, "I wish this cursed box would open!"

The words were barely past her lips when she stopped moving altogether. She stared at Yi for so long it made the young girl nervous.

"What it is, your Highness?"

Ling didn't answer. She stood up and looked toward

the gate of the garden leading to the city's plaza and the long line of people with boxes still standing, then to the ground, then slowly up the roots, trunk, branches and fruit of the tree they were sitting under. There she saw a peach gently swaying in the breeze.

"Your Highness?" Yi inquired.

Still in silence, the Princess knelt down in the grass and gently lifted the box once more. She held it close to her lips and whispered: "Great souls rely on their wills; weak ones have only wishes."

Immediately the pieces of wood that composed the box began moving on their own. The girls' eyes and mouths opened in amazement. The pieces of wood fell away one by one, finally exposing a beautiful, peach wood box with the most intricate carving of a peach tree on it's lid.

With Yi looking on, Princess Lingxiao slowly opened the box to expose a perfect peach pit within. The girls looked at each other, wide-eyed with smiles transforming their faces.

Yi swallowed, trying to find her voice. "What do we wish for?"

Ling was way ahead of her. She was already nodding, "I know. May I?"

"It is your present, Princess," Yi told her, "You do with it as you wish."

"It will be for the both of us," Ling said as she clasped Yi's little hands in her own and closed her eyes. "We wish... We wish to dance on air."

Before the words were finished, the girls were lifted off the ground. They both shrieked with excitement. Ling took hold of Yi's hand and waist and spun her around. Yi threw her head back and laughed and laughed.

"Higher," Ling demanded, and up they rose above the tree. They shrieked again, looking down at the ground below, frightened but excited, spinning and twirling and laughing out loud.

"Higher, higher, higher," the Princess demanded. The dancing girls spun their way up and up until the castle and city below looked like toys.

If you've never felt the happiness of dancing without a care you cannot know the sheer joy that Princess Lingxiao experienced that day. Not only could she float across the floor as she did on earth but this floor had no hard surface to land on, nor walls to contain her, nor ceiling to limit how high she could leap. She could spin till she was dizzy, dive into a cushion of air or jump upwards toward the sun. It was magnificent.

"Higher," Ling demanded. Yi's heart was in her throat as the girls rose so high they could almost touch the clouds.

"Please, Princess, this is high enough," Yi said growing fearful.

Maybe Ling had never heard the tale about flying too high and falling because of wings made of feathers and wax. Or maybe the story wasn't told in her part of the world. Or perhaps she just didn't care about anything except getting more and more of this glorious feeling.

"Higher!" she demanded in spite of Yi's warning, and up they went above the clouds.

No one had flown before so no one could have known what happens when you reach that height and therefore no one could have warned the Princess that the air is too thin to breath so far above the earth. Your head goes dizzy, your brain confuses and without the air you need... you faint away. That's what happened to the girls.

They fainted and they began to fall.

The fall was so far that after a few moments, Yi started coming to her senses. She saw what was happening and screamed. She shook the Princess to wake her. Ling opened her eyes but was so groggy she couldn't focus. It seemed like a dream to her.

"You must wake up, your highness. We will die!" Yi yelled to her. But Ling did not respond.

She watched Yi as if in a dream, below her with the earth farther away but growing closer, faster and faster. She frowned as the young girl grabbed hold of the sides of her flowing gown, bunching the material together.

As the Princess watched in her dreamlike state, she thought, "Look at her working to save us both. Poor people must be so much smarter about survival than I am. When they're faced with death they don't lose their heads. Maybe it's because they face danger and starvation almost daily. What brave souls they are."

After several moments, Yi had created a sort of parachute out of Princess Ling's massive dress – although no one had ever heard of one back then. Suddenly it caught the air and they floated down, not speeding toward their certain death. "This is much nicer," the Princess thought. Then she hit the ground, banged her head and everything became dark.

When Ling opened her eyes she was staring at the blue sky. "It's so pretty," she said to no one. "I should look at it more often."

When she sat up, she was still in the garden, next to the peach tree. The wooden box was by her side, fully restored to its original, plain, ugly form. Yi was nowhere to be seen. Where had she gone?

Ling ran to the entrance of the garden to ask the guards if they had seen the young lady who had been with her?

"We saw no one with you as you entered, Your Highness," one Guard replied

"The little beggar girl who's been with me all afternoon," the Princess said.

The other Guard agreed with the first. "You have been alone all afternoon, Princess. No one else entered or left."

"That's impossible!" Ling told them. "Find the beggar girl now! Her name is Yi."

"Yes, Your Highness," they responded, as one ran into the garden and the other into the streets to search.

Lingxiao's head was reeling. Where did she go? What happened? She still felt a bit dizzy so she retired to her bedroom and slept through till morning.

When she woke she couldn't remember if the whole thing had been a dream or not. Yet there was the ugly wooden box by her side.

She checked with the Guards and was told that Yi was

nowhere to be found.

Ling took Guards with her and searched the city looking for her friend. They looked everywhere and asked everyone if they had seen her. As the afternoon light was fading an Old Man said he knew of such a girl and pointed them to the marketplace.

The Princess was so excited when she saw the young Beggar Girl. "Oh, Yi, I've been looking everywhere for you..." she said as the Girl turned and looked at her. The Girl did have a face very much like Yi's but, alas, it wasn't her. You'd think that Ling would be heartbroken, but somehow she wasn't.

Somehow finding even a trace of her friend in the stranger's face made her happy. It brought a smile to her face and she reached out and held the Girl's hand. The Princess decided then and there to befriend this Beggar Girl and she brought the Girl and her family to the castle to live with her.

The next day Ling went out again to search for Yi - this time with the little Beggar Girl by her side. As they passed the garden the Girl said, "Oh, peaches! May I have one?"

"Of course," the Princess said. "We will fill a basket!"

They gathered up all the peaches they could carry and traveled the city with the Guards. Each time they came across a beggar girl, they gave her a peach and coins to feed and clothe her and pay for a decent place to live.

For months Ling and the Beggar Girl searched throughout the city and then the surrounding villages but there was no word, no trace of Yi. They came upon many poor, beggar girls and gave them each a peach and money from the Royal coffers.

In time, they did the same for every unfortunate person they met: girls and boys, young and old.

The King brought his daughter before him and told her that she was spending far too much of their money and that she must stop. Ling knelt before the King and said to him simply, "Your Majesty, I know it isn't right to disobey you, but if I must, I will sell all that I have to continue this work. Father, I can't - I *won't* stop."

The King reached down and took his daughter's delicate face in his hand. He couldn't decide if he was more proud of her for her determination or for her giving heart. "Of course, my daughter," he said. "You must continue"

In this way Princess Lingxiao became the fulfillment of the legend of The Wooden Box, for she represented Hope to the poor people of her kingdom.

THE END

Chaderick Adams'

The Prince
Who Never Cleaned His Room

By
Marc Clark

PF

Our story begins in a time before there were phones and electricity, before engines and machinery, before most of the things you see around you or depend on to live your life were ever invented. This much I know.

I can't know for sure where you are when you hear this story. You may be in the exact spot where it took place. Anything is possible... as you will see.

There once was a kingdom where the sun burned so brightly that the heat made it impossible to work when it was highest in the sky. The people would find shade and rest during those hours, then go back to their jobs when the heat subsided. They called that rest a siesta.

The sun was so strong that most of the homes and the castle itself were bleached white to reflect the heat.

They say that there is something about that kind of heat that makes the blood run hotter; tempers smolder, passions flare and hearts burst into flame. That's how it was for the King and Queen.

From the moment he saw her, he fell madly and deeply in love - as she did with him. He was a young Prince, she a Princess. They stole away every chance they could. Any moment they could be together, they would take it: ducking into doorways just to steal a kiss; escaping into the gardens after the castle was asleep and talking till the sun came up.

After they took the throne their passion never faded.

They were one of those annoying couples that are always kissing. They'd have terrible arguments about nothing important and then when they made up (which they always did) they did it in style: throwing themselves a lavish party and spending the evening "ooo-ing" and "ahh-ing" over each other.

It wasn't long after they became King and Queen that they gave birth to a baby boy. They named him, Feliciano – which means joy or festivity - because he was so happy that he lit up their lives. He was a non-stop, all day, every day bundle of joy.

As a baby he would giggle and grab at everything, his eyes wide open from the moment he woke till the second he fell asleep at night (no naps for him). As a toddler he would run through the hallways with a nursemaid in hot pursuit, climbing stairs and furniture and scaring the life out of the entire Royal Staff. By the age of six no one could keep up with him; by eight no one knew how to teach him; by ten he was possibly the only one in the kingdom who was running around during siesta. So the King and Queen decided to do something about this unstoppable Prince.

They figured they could look at the problem one of two ways: either the child couldn't concentrate on anything for an extended period of time so they'd have to force him into a system to be like everyone else; or, that the world wasn't quite moving fast enough to hold the child's attention and, instead, his studies would have to be fashioned to fit his pace. Since Feliciano was a Prince, his parents decided to mold his education to suit him.

Each day they had two professors ready at all times in case one or the other couldn't hold the Prince's focus. There was also an instructor who could teach combat, fencing or dance so he could get some much needed physical activity. As soon as Feliciano's attention started to drift, the next teacher would step in.

What they found was that because he remained so sharp and so focused he excelled at practically everything. He learned several languages in less than half the time others could, along with math, the sciences and history. He became an excellent swordsman, gymnast and dancer practically overnight. There was almost nothing the young Prince couldn't accomplish working at three times the pace of any other child his age.

That's not to say that Feliciano was great at everything.

He was not too good at keeping himself clean. He couldn't sit still long enough for others to bathe him and on his own he moved so fast that he'd always miss a few places: there'd be smudges on his face, his feet might stink and lots of time he'd forget to wash his hair altogether – much less comb it.

Dressing himself... that didn't go too well. You could count on at least one or two buttons remaining unbuttoned, a sock missing, two different shoes or his shirt inside out.

Sitting still for a meal also proved too tough for him. He always seemed to be running through the halls eating fruit or a piece of pie that was dripping all over him. He couldn't stay seated during meals so he'd visit everyone else and eat from their plates while telling them fantastic stories that no one was ever sure were true. He'd grab a piece of cheese from one plate and tell the owner a tale about a Shepherd in the South who had a sheep born with two heads, but the heads could never agree on anything, so it ended up walking off a cliff because it couldn't make up its minds which way to go. When he'd take a sip from someone's cup he'd explain how a vineyard in the hills produced a wine of such strength that those who drank it found themselves waking up in the streets the next morning without a stitch of clothing on! People in the town complained until, finally, they made a law that from now on only newlyweds would be allowed to buy it. Nobody minded sharing their food with the Prince because he was so much fun to have around.

The one thing that the King and Queen were very firm about was that their son had to keep his room clean. The room didn't have to be perfect but it did have to be neat and tidy. Yes, he had servants to do that, but they felt it was important that one area of his personal life be his responsibility. They also knew (although they didn't tell the Prince) that it would be impossible for him to keep a wife happy because no woman likes to live with a slob – even a Princely one.

He could do a fast sweeping, a quick dusting, a hurried picking up and putting away of clothing and he would be done. If he did that once a day before lunch it wouldn't take too long and it would make a world of difference.

"Of course I can do that," Feliciano told his parents. He believed it, too. And he actually did exactly that… for, maybe… two and half days. Halfway through the third day the young Prince was sweeping a corner and a spider ran across his feet so he placed the broom handle in its path and it scurried around it. He placed his foot as an obstacle and the spider hopped over it. He chased the insect across the room putting up roadblocks of tables, chairs, shoes and the like until it zoomed out of reach under his bed in the corner of the room.

Just then the bells rang announcing lunch and he just didn't have any more time to clean, did he? So he took the stockings and shirt that were laying on his table and chair and tossed them under the bed, and decided to use the broom to do a fast dusting. That didn't prove to be too great an idea because he knocked over a candle and broke the candleholder. He swept those under the bed as well and took a look around at the room. "Done," he claimed with satisfaction and ran off down the stairs.

It wasn't such a terrible thing, but the fact is, when you sweep your problems under the bed they're still there when you wake up.

The next day, the Prince had every intention of cleaning out the stuff from under his bed, and he wanted to experiment with his new broom-dusting discovery from the day before. So he tied his dirty shirt to the end of the broom and sort of "swept-dusted" the entire place. Which worked out great - if you don't count the fact that he ruined his shirt, knocked a picture off the wall, broke it and swept it all under the bed, then forgot about the time because he started dancing around the room with his broom as a partner and again had to run off to lunch after tossing his dirty clothes under the bed.

It didn't stop there. It never does. Bad habits are like a deep hole; once you fall into them it's hard to get out. So anytime Feliciano didn't have enough time to clean his room properly he'd toss a shirt, a shoe or an odd sock under the bed; he'd sweep dirt, bugs and leftover food under it; the game he hadn't quite finished; the book he was supposed to read; the orange he meant to eat for breakfast. Any cake he was eating the night before that he left on his nightstand? – the next morning he'd slide what was left over under the bed.

Now and then he'd search the growing pile for a missing shoe or shirt but for the most part he'd just stuff more and more and more things under there. For weeks this went on. Then months.

As you can guess, this was a massive bed. Much larger than what we call king-size. For the Royal Family, craftsmen would make extra large oak bed frames because they didn't have standard sized mattresses back then. They didn't even have mattresses, really. They filled a huge bag with straw – which they would switch out when it got stale or smelly – and then put another, thinner bag filled with feathers on top of that.

The pile was getting bigger and bigger and even sticking out in places so now and then the Prince would kick it with his feet to jam it in tighter. It also started to smell a little so Feliciano asked for scented candles to mask the stench.

Bugs were attracted to the mix of food and mold and garbage under the Prince's bed, but then a lizard or two showed up and solved the bug problem. "Life solves its own problems," the Prince thought to himself – which made no sense at all but made him feel good anyway.

Feliciano did chase a mouse around the room one afternoon and it probably made a comfortable nest in the mess.

When the Prince heard scratching noises in the night he would write it off to a nice little mouse family going about its business.

This went on for… well, for about as long as something wrong like this can go on: the smell got to be too much, the pile got so big that it couldn't be stuffed back in and the Prince started showing up with bites from an insect that no one could identify.

It's surprising how long you can live with something when you know it's wrong. You put on blinders and keep going until your mistakes are right there in front of you, sticking out from under your bed.

The Prince ran up the stairs to his bedroom to do his "cleaning" before lunch and found his parents, the King and Queen, standing in the room waiting for him. To say they weren't exactly happy would be an understatement. Neither of them was well known for keeping their tempers and they weren't about to start now.

They yelled and screamed at the young Prince about how he didn't do what he said he would, how he lied to them and turned his beautiful bedroom into a garbage dump. They were so upset that if there had been anything left in his room that he hadn't already broken while cleaning up, they would have broken it for him.

As hurt and scared and sorry as Feliciano was, he was relieved to have it done with. He was tired of the guilt and mess. It felt like he had been keeping a dark secret and he wasn't a big fan of darkness or secrets – he preferred the truth and the sunlight.

"I am sorry I disappointed you, your Majesties," he told them when they finally stopped screaming. "I disappointed myself as well."

The King and Queen wanted to hug their little boy at that moment, but they kept their stern demeanors and told him that he would be locked in his room until it was completely spotless.

"Of course, your Majesties. That's only fair," the Prince said, trying not to cry.

His parents hurried from the room before their son's sadness brought tears to their own eyes. They had servants bring cleaning supplies and trashcans to Feliciano's room and lock him in.

*****

The first hour or two it was mostly the young Prince pulling one thing at a time out from under the bed and being miserable: a dirty, dusty pair of pants, his unfinished drawings of a horse he had seen running through the orchards, a broken piece of the frame that held his mother's painting, that shoe he'd been looking for…

The servants listening outside the door couldn't take it after awhile. They were so used to laughter coming from the happy Prince, to hear him sighing and moaning and crying broke their hearts. And he certainly couldn't be allowed to starve, so they left a tray of meats and cheeses inside the door, locked it and left.

The young Prince had to hold his breath as he dug through gross, moldy clothing, spider webs, mouse droppings and the thick cover of dirt that had formed on the floor. He even found an unopened present he'd received for his birthday a month before. He was excited until he saw that the box had been chewed through on one corner and whatever had been inside was gone – some kind of sweets probably - and in its place... Well, I guess the only gifts you get when you mess up really bad are full of... umm, mouse droppings.

He was a little more than halfway through clearing out the bed and already the trashcans were mostly full and he'd shoveled out piles of dirt. "Where does all the dirt come from?" he wondered aloud. "Is it an 'ashes to ashes, dust to dust, dirt to dirt' kind of thing?" Then he pulled out what looked like a small animal skeleton. He got so scared he bumped his head on the bottom of the bed as he scrambled out from under it, then scooted across the floor to the opposite wall.

"What the heck was that?" he wondered, breathing hard.

Suddenly there was a loud metallic scratching on the floor. He let out a scream and pressed himself further against the wall, trying to get as far away from the bed as he could.

Then he heard what sounded like a muffled voice. He stared at the bed. He was sure it said his name: "Prince Feliciano." Whatever it was, it could talk!

Just then there was a knock on the door and the Prince realized that the voice wasn't coming from under the bed at all. He looked over in the fading light and saw that his dinner tray was being set down just inside the door, which would account for the metal scratching. He relaxed and laughed at himself.

"Are you alright, your Highness?" the voice from the other side of the door asked. It was his servant, Alejandro.

"I'm fine," Feliciano yelled back as he got to his feet.

"Are you almost done, my Prince?" the voice asked. "I wish I could spare you this effort."

"I'm sure I'll be done by morning, Alejandro. It's my mess to clean up," he told him as he lit a candle. "Sometimes you make the right decision, other times you have to make decisions right."

The Prince sat on the floor eating his dinner, staring at the bed in the corner. He'd lit all of the candles and lanterns but he still didn't want to go under the bed again. He realized what the skeleton had been. It was a lizard - a fairly large one. What could have eaten a lizard?

Just then something under the bed shifted around and Feliciano jumped. Something large was under there. He put the meat he was eating in his pocket while his other hand quietly reached for the broom. He aimed the broom handle at the bed as if it was a spear. Then the huge bed lifted off the ground and slammed back down!

Feliciano raced to the door and banged on it as loud as he could. "Alejandro! There's something in here! Alejandro! Anyone!" When he got no response, he figured there wouldn't be any help – probably not until the morning.

Again the bed lifted off the ground and slammed to the floor! Whatever was under there had to be big and very powerful.

The Prince removed his small dagger, the only weapon he had. It would likely be too small to do any real damage to whatever was under the four-poster so he used it to sharpen the end of the broom handle into a spear.

He came up with a plan.

First he tossed the meat he had in his pocket to the far side of the bed to distract the thing. He watched as the bed was dragged a few inches toward the food. Then he quietly climbed on top of the bed from the other side. He figured it would be best to surprise whatever it was and stab it if it ever came out into the room.

Well, it did!

All he could see at first was a huge thick mass of knotted, coarse, grey hair. The Prince knew enough about combat to strike first – most fights are settled with the first blow – so he raised his broomstick spear and brought it down with all his might.

The beast was incredibly fast. It dodged to one side while twisting its ugly head upward and bit the broomstick, snapping it in pieces.

That's when Feliciano saw that it was rat - a giant one, at least five times the normal size. If you've never seen one, rats are about as ugly as they come – giant ones are even uglier: a drooling mouth full of razor-sharp teeth and blank, dead, black eyes.

The Prince fell backward as the giant rat lunged at him. In one move he rolled over onto the floor and ran. The massive rodent dug its long claws into the bed and jumped on top of it after him.

Feliciano scrambled onto the top of his dresser just as the beast rammed its head into it. The rat backed up and hit it again and again until the dresser toppled and the Prince hopped to the floor and ran as fast as he could to the wardrobe – the tall wooden closet - and he jumped up and caught hold of the top of it, just barely.

The rat barreled toward him as he tried to pull himself up, slamming into the side of the wooden closet, dislodging one of the Prince's hands.

Hanging by only one hand, he watched the relentless rodent rise up on its hind legs, showing its dripping fangs, about to attack. He pulled with all of his strength. Grabbing hold with his other hand he got high enough off the ground to avoid getting his feet bitten clean off!

The Prince climbed on to the top of the wardrobe and held on with both hands, wrapping his legs around it, too. He watched the huge, ugly beast back up again and again and again and ram itself into the wardrobe, tipping it further and further each time. It wouldn't be long until he knocked it over or damaged it so severely that it collapsed.

The young Prince was very smart – not smart enough to have known that an animal could grow under his bed – but smart. He knew enough about rats to know that their vision wasn't too great. They find their way mostly by sensing movement, sound and especially by smell. So - and this wasn't easy - the Prince started ripping his clothes off: bam!, the giant rat hit the wardrobe as he got his shirt off; bam!, again as he got his stockings off; bam!, once more as he tried to get out of his pants and the wardrobe crashed to the ground.

Feliciano covered his head as the giant piece of furniture crumbled around him. It took him a moment to get his bearings but the giant rodent was already tearing through the wreckage after him. His pants were caught on a heavy piece of wood so he sliced them off with his dagger.

He turned and saw the rat was almost on top of him so he drove the dagger into its head.

The beast screamed and spun around in circles trying to remove the blade. Taking his chance, the Prince scrambled to his feet and moved around his bedroom, dropping pieces of clothing everywhere to distract the beast. He grabbed a trashcan and poured it over himself to mask his scent and carried another with him to the bed, thinking that the smells from the straw, the feathers and the garbage would throw the rodent off.

As the Prince suspected, the dagger didn't stop the rodent, -- it only slowed him down. When it realized it couldn't pull the knife from its head it re-doubled its effort to find the person who stabbed it. The rat scurried around the room shredding every piece of clothing that the Prince left behind. When they were all in pieces, the beast went up on its hind legs, sniffing the air for a human scent. Its ears and whiskers twitched, listening and feeling for some type of movement.

Feliciano sat, perfectly still, barely breathing, knowing the slightest movement would be the end of him. He stayed that way as minutes dragged into hours. He didn't dare sleep - he couldn't anyway - because the giant rat continually scoured the room, so he occupied his mind with figuring out how this could have happened: just as the lizards had been attracted by the insects and the mice had been attracted by the leftover food, the bugs, amphibians and animals had attracted the rat. Who knows how long it had been under there, feeding and growing. It was frightening to think of but fear keeps you sharp and that's what Feliciano needed, now more than ever.

It's funny, the young Prince had barely stopped moving from the moment he was born and now he had to sit for hours without moving a muscle.

Suddenly there was a knock on the door. The rat immediately scurried toward the sound and crouched ready to attack.

"Your Majesty, are you through with your meal? Can I do anything to help?" Alejandro yelled from beyond the door.

"Oh, no!" the Prince thought to himself. If he yelled back the rat would come after him. If he said nothing, Alejandro would come in and the rodent would attack him instead.

It didn't matter because before he could think of what to do he heard the key in the door.

"Alejandro. Pull your sword!" Feliciano yelled.

Everything happened at once: the rat turned and rushed toward the bed and the sound of his voice; the Prince got up, grabbing the covers and sheets as he did; his servant pushed open the door with his sword drawn.

The giant rodent jumped onto the bed and flew at Feliciano. The Prince sidestepped and covered the beast with the bedding.

As the rat ripped his way through the cloth Feliciano yelled out, "Alejandro, your blade!" His servant tossed him his broadsword and the Prince caught it just as the massive rodent tore itself free.

In one move, Feliciano sliced upward from the rat's underbelly to his throat and the giant rodent fell to the floor, dead.

It was over, just like that.

The Prince sank to the floor: shaking, bloody and exhausted. His servant covered him with a robe, amazed at what had transpired.

*****

From that day forward the Prince still rushed around from place to place, from lesson to lesson and was the only person in the kingdom that you could hear running through the streets during siesta time. He still went from seat to seat during meals telling fantastic stories (though they did seem a bit more believable after the tale of the giant rat got out). But you can be sure that he never ever let his room get dirty again: in fact, the space under his bed remained spotless until the day he died.

THE END

Alekzy Alana Rodriquez'

The Princess
Who Was Very, Very Organized

By
Marc Clark

PF

Chapter I

If seconds were years then this story would have happened merely hours ago. But they aren't and it didn't.

If inches stretched for miles then this story could have happened just down the street from you. But they don't and it didn't.

Walk out your door and travel back through the centuries. Instead of the homes or buildings surrounding you, picture a gleaming, white and turquoise castle with jeweled steeples and doves circling in an endless flight pattern, surrounded by an expansive city with white walls and massive iron gates that open every morning at dawn to expose the sounds and smells of a plaza filled with peddlers and merchants. Then climb the wide, marble stairs to the entrance of the royal house where golden doors open to allow you into a palace which only a select few ever see: the opulence of the Great Hall, the entrance to the Royal Chamber where court is held, the dual alabaster staircases leading to the bedrooms of the King and Queen, a hallway lined with the rooms of the many Princes and Princesses and finally around the corner, to the smallest of the bedrooms belonging to the youngest Princess: Princess Niloufar.

She was so named because the Princess had emerged from her mother's womb, stretching her arms as if she were greeting the morning sun - which had just appeared through the open windows. Niloufar, or Nilou as they called her, means Morning Glory, and she was indeed a glory on that morning.

Parents will tell you that some babies are difficult while others are no trouble at all. You'll hear some complain that they never get any sleep because the child is always fussing, others will bend the ear of anyone who will listen about how their baby sleeps through the night, naps regularly and plays alone for hours. It doesn't mean the children grow up with the same traits. Sometimes the opposite is true.

Well, Nilou was one of those perfect children: bright and happy, crawling into her bed to sleep without any encouragement and constantly busying herself with toys – she would even put them away when she was done.

She didn't change much at all as she grew, either: as soon as she learned to walk she figured out how to put on her own shoes, and placed them neatly back in her wardrobe when she was done for the day; as soon as she learned to talk she concentrated intently on the speaker and kept repeating a word until she said it perfectly; whatever she was taught by her instructors she committed to memory and took it upon herself to study the lessons ahead. If there had been "extra credit" for royalty she would have certainly received it. (There wasn't, by the way.)

As a little girl the Princess became the fast favorite of the entire Royal Staff: she kept her things and her room spotless, leaving the housemaids very little to do; she cleaned her plate at every meal without dirtying the linen to the delight of the cooks and servers; and what nursemaid wouldn't love a young girl who bathed and dressed herself without being told?

Though her behavior seemed perfect when Nilou was

little, as she got older it did start to become, well, kind of annoying. How would you like to be the housemaid who is daily walked around every inch of the Princess's room as she points out each tiny speck of dust, a doll whose little dress isn't pressed properly or, heaven forbid , that there would be an insect in the room. (The windows didn't have glass in them - what would you expect?) Or imagine the chef and server who had to cook all of Nilou's meals individually to her specifications where only certain colors could go together, where vegetables had to be cut to the exact same size and none of the food on the plate was *ever* allowed to touch or the Princess would send it back and they would have to start from scratch.

And you probably know, if you have brothers and sisters, usually there's one child who's considered "the perfect one.". They always do everything right and blah, blah, blah. The other kids in the family grow to resent them and avoid them and exclude them whenever possible. That's how the other Princes and Princesses felt toward Nilou. I mean, how many dinners had been ruined because of her pickiness and how many times were dances or outings delayed because the drapes clashed with her dress or the carriages didn't have the proper ribbons attached to the horses' manes? Who notices that stuff, anyway?

Plus, when things didn't go as planned, if everything wasn't in its correct place at the correct time in the correct manner the Little Princess would throw an unmanageable, unbelievable hissy fit! Do you know what a "hissy fit" is? Well, it's pretty much what you'd imagine when you put the words "hissy" and "fit" together. Trust me, you don't want to see one.

Now before you go and start feeling the same way

about Princess Niloufar as her brothers and sisters and staff felt, let me explain something. She didn't choose to be like that. She didn't plan it. It was something that, early on in her life, gave her a great deal of comfort, so why wouldn't she keep doing it? Later, it became all she knew and it frightened her to have anything out of place – it meant the world wasn't right somehow. She got to a point where she was scared to death of anything that wasn't organized. So, before you judge someone, keep in mind that many people do what they do because they're afraid; afraid of change, mostly.

*****

The day it all started to fall apart for the Princess began like every other day. I mean, every single day began in exactly the same way.

Nilou would open her eyes as soon as the rooster crowed. She then sat up and placed her feet into the soft slippers positioned perfectly on the floor next to her bed and put on the robe that was placed perfectly at the foot of her bed. She washed her face the same way every day with the same sized piece of soap laid out the night before. She opened her wardrobe the same way, right door, then left, scanned and then chose one of the perfectly pressed dresses hanging on the handmade hangers, hemmed to exactly the same length, arranged by color with matching shoes sitting directly below and matching veils directly above. She chose perfectly matching rings and baubles arranged in her perfectly clean, perfectly organized jewelry box that contained every piece of jewelry she ever received, polished every day to sparkle like new. She styled her hair in exactly the same, perfectly coiffed way. She would wrap her headdress around her head and attach the veil so that it would drape perfectly across her face. At breakfast she was served the same, perfectly prepared fruits and breads. She attended her singing lesson and her voice was pitch perfect. She attended her dancing lessons and her moves were perfectly choreographed. But when she sat down to eat her perfectly prepared lunch her father, the King, announced that she was to travel to the Southern castle for the Spring and perfect Princess Niloufar spit out her tea all over the table in shock!

There's nothing the Princess disliked more than traveling. Day trips were fine because she could organize the whole thing, but long distances... she wouldn't have her bed and slippers ready, her wardrobe and jewelry cases laid out perfectly – all the things that made her life so safe and so perfect. And then there was the dust and dirt and rain and smells. Nilou shrieked out loud just thinking about it, scaring everyone at the table.

Remember that hissy fit I told you about? That's what happened next. The other Princes and Princesses had seen it before so they grabbed their food and drink and ran off to another room. The servants and servers ducked back into the kitchen. The King and Queen sat there, patiently, until their daughter wore herself out from crying and screaming and banging her head and stomping her feet.

With tears still streaming down her face, she begged and pleaded with her father to let her stay at home but he would have none of it. Getting his daughter to venture out into the world would do her good, he thought, so he was firm in his decision.

The Princess screamed, "I won't go! I won't. I won't, I won't, I won't!" and stomped off to her room, throwing herself on the bed - not caring at all that the cover hadn't been turned down exactly right or even that she was getting tears on her freshly washed coverlet - until she sobbed herself to sleep.

She was really not happy.

*****

The trip was just as long and miserable as the Princess had imagined. The first day was all dust and heat and being jostled around in a carriage. She did manage to pack all of her favorite jewelry and dresses and slippers and veils. They were all bouncing beside her as the caravan made its way up the mountain path.

Although she was given a beautiful silken tent to rest in for the night she thought it was the most awful thing she could think of and she cried herself to sleep, yearning for the comfort of her fluffy, perfect bed.

That night the rains started and they continued the next day - and they just wouldn't stop. Torrential, endless rain. What could be worse? The caravan was moving so slowly, slogging through the mud, up a mountain road. Ugh, she hated mud. "Why would anyone invent mud," she thought. "Euww."

Then her carriage stopped abruptly. "Now what?" she said, trying to look out the window without getting wet. "What is it?" she yelled out the window at no one in particular.

She heard loud voices and horses neighing. Servants and soldiers were rushing by her carriage, yelling and giving orders. Then she heard a mountainous rumbling and crashing, shaking the carriage and throwing her from her seat. She was so mad. Now her hair was a mess, plus all of her belongings were tossed onto the floor.

A large Soldier appeared at the carriage door. "Are you alright, Princess?"

"No, I'm not alright. Get my carriage away from this place. I don't want any more disturbances," she told him sharply.

The Soldier opened the door and reached in for her. "You must leave now, your Highness."

She slapped his hands away, saying, "I am doing no such thing and get your hands away from me!"

The large man adjusted his thinking and spoke quickly but plainly to Nilou, reasoning with her. "You are in grave danger, Princess. The rains have softened the mountain and mudslides have taken out most of the road. We fear that the bridge we are standing on will fall into the ravine. To save your life you must come now and bring nothing with you."

She could see the fear and desperation in the Soldier's demeanor but leaving her things was even more frightening to her. "There is no chance that I will leave my-" – the next thing out of her mouth was a terrible scream because the rocky wall behind the Soldier's head burst open with a river of water and completely engulfed him, washing him away and drenching the inside of the carriage. Her screams continued as the force of the water turned the carriage on its side, crashing it onto the wooden bridge.

The soldiers scrambled to get the horses to their feet but the rains forced one after the other off the bridge and into the ravine below. Suddenly the wooden structure cracked like thunder and began to break into pieces.

The Royal Family, soldiers and servants watched in horror from the other side of the bridge as Nilou's carriage was swept up in a river of mud from the mountaintop. The Queen shrieked as the bridge collapsed under the weight and slid down, down, down into the ravine.

They had no time to see how and where the Princess's carriage landed or if she had survived because the mud and rock of the mountain continued to come down around them. It was all they could do to ride down the mountain trail as fast as the horses could carry them, away from the muddy river, - away from the Princess, leaving her behind.

All but one: a stable boy, Anoush.

He knew it was hopeless; that he could never make it down the ravine, and even if he did, what chance would he have of getting to the other side of the ravine and finding the Princess in all of the mud and water and devastation?

Still, he pulled on the reigns of his horse, bringing it to a stop. With the rain drenching and mud inching up around the horse's hooves, he remembered his father telling him to always judge the situation and if you are more likely to come to harm than to profit from a solution, don't attempt it. His mother, however, simply said, "Feel what is in your heart, my son, and you will always follow the right path."

Anoush turned his horse around and they both trudged up the mountain. When they finally reached the top where the bridge once stood he let the horse go and stared down into the ravine.

He had only seen the Princess one time, over a year ago, returning from an outing in the countryside, but he recalled every detail of her eyes - how the sunlight made them sparkle - and the deep green color that matched her veil and headdress. He remembered her flowing hair, and the grace of her hand on the carriage door. He had never seen such beauty mixed with so much sadness. She smiled and appeared to be enjoying herself but there was no joy in her joyfulness.

He'd barely started his climb down when the rocks fell away under his feet. He was sliding down fast. He dug the balls of his feet into the side of the mountain, trying to get a footing but he kept sliding down faster. He clawed at the rocks with his fingers as he fell even faster and faster. Suddenly his feet caught a ledge and he stopped, breathing heavily, hugging the side of the mountain with the mud pouring down on his head. His feet and hands were cut and bleeding.

The ravine fell off another hundred feet to a rocky riverbed. If he hadn't stopped, his body would have ended up there, crushed and broken. He looked down. There were no remnants of the carriage.

Anoush made his way across part of the demolished bridge to the other side of the ravine and tracked the path of where the carriage would have fallen. All he saw was mud, rock and broken timber. Where could it be?

Then he saw something at his feet, protruding from the mud: a thin, purple piece of cloth. He dug it out. It was the Princess's veil. He turned to look at the mountain of mud behind him and started digging with his hands as fast as he could, pulling away rock and debris.

A corner of the carriage roof appeared and he dug faster and faster until he found the window.

He could see inside. It was half filled with mud. The Princess was there – the upper part of her body anyway - her head drooped, her hair covered her face. He couldn't tell if she was alive or not.

He kept digging. A large boulder was wedged against the door. It was probably what stopped the carriage from falling all the way down the ravine. He couldn't open the door to reach the Princess unless he moved it out of the way.

Anoush wedged his body between the carriage and the huge rock and pushed the boulder with his legs little by little, then gave it one big shove that sent it rolling down the mountain.

He pulled open the door and mud flowed out of the carriage and Nilou's body fell into his arms. He looked down at her, watching the raindrops trying to rinse clean her delicate face. Her large green eyes opened and looked up at him. "I have come for you, Princess," he said.

"Huh? Who are you?" she said, trying to get an idea of what was going on.

"My name is Anoush, your Highness. We must go," he told her, clearing the mud from her legs. "We don't have much time."

The Princess had no idea what was happening. She kept looking around. She pulled one of her dresses out of the mud. "My dress! Look what you've done! Ahhh! I hate mud!"

There was a huge, deep, creaking sound as the entire carriage shifted several inches.

"Now! We must go now!" Anoush yelled as he pulled the Princess's feet from out of the mud.

"My things. You must get my jewelry, my dresses. I cannot forget my veils, certainly," she told him as she reached around in the mud.

This time the sound was like crunching wood and bending metal. The roof of the carriage started lowering from the weight of the mud pressing down from above while the whole thing starting sliding. "Now, your Highness!" Anoush yelled, grabbing her by the waist.

She pounded his shoulders with both of her little

hands screaming into his face, "I need my things!"

Anoush held her with one arm and reached back into the carriage as the roof creaked lower and lower and the whole thing slid farther toward edge of the cliff. His free arm scrambled through the mud, desperate to find something, anything, as the Princess yelled over and over: "I need my things! I need my things!" like a little child.

He found a large box and pulled it out. "Here!" he yelled, handing it to her.

"Thank you," she said as the roof caved in and a rush of mud and rock and water heaved the carriage.

Anoush dove out of the way at the last moment, holding Nilou who was clutching the box. They fell into the mud and turned to watch the carriage roll over and over down the ravine, splitting into pieces until there was nothing left of it.

The stable boy looked over at the Princess sitting in the mud with her muddy box held tightly to her chest. She took in a breath and started to cry. He felt so sorry for the sad, beautiful, little girl. She turned to him, with tears and raindrops running down her cheeks. "My dresses," she said through her sobs. Then she stared down at the wreckage below. "Now what am I going to wear?"

Chapter II

To Princess Niloufar it felt as though they had been trudging through the mud and rain for weeks. The truth was it had only been about a half an hour (she wasn't used to walking). He had carried her and her box in his arms for the journey down the slope to level ground, helped her over rocks and picked her up again when the terrain was too difficult.

They hadn't spoken the whole time. Nilou was too devastated by the loss of her perfect world, watching all of her perfect things crashing to pieces before her very eyes. It was too much. The rain was letting up now and the skies were beginning to show signs of blue, but the mud – the mud just would not end. "This is what Hell must be like," she imagined. "No. If it was, it would have kept on raining."

She looked at the soaked, muddy, poorly dressed young man walking ahead of her. He must be about fifteen years old, she thought.

"Who are you again?" she asked him.

"My name is Anoush, your Highness."

"Alright. That doesn't really help," she told him. "Did my father send you to rescue me?"

"No, your Highness."

"The Captain of the Guards?"

"No, your Highness. It's just me," he told her.

"You don't look like a soldier."

He stopped and turned to look at her. "No, I… I work in the stables, your Highness."

Nilou stopped in her tracks and stared at him, open-mouthed. "Excuse me?" she said. "Wha… Shouldn't you have a horse or something?" She put her hand to her forehead, trying to figure out what she was hearing. "I really don't understand what happened."

Anoush motioned for her to sit on a nearby boulder, which she did. He set down the box and explained it this way: "The bridge we were crossing was destroyed by a mudslide. Many were killed."

She gasped. "My parents? My family?"

"I cannot say, Princess. I believe they are well. We watched from one side of the ravine as the bridge fell. Your carriage was on the other side and it was swept down the mountain. If we had stayed, we all would have perished. What was left of the caravan retreated down the mountain to safety. The Royal Family included."

"But not you?" she asked.

"I did start off with the rest…" Anoush said and drifted off.

"But you came back." Nilou finished for him. He nodded. "For me?" He nodded again.

The Princess stood up, thinking this over. She looked at the poor stable boy. She had never seen him before and yet he risked his life for her. Why? It didn't make any sense.

"Well… thank you," she said (pretty much because she didn't know what else to say).

Anoush didn't know what to say either so he just nodded again.

They both tried to think of what else to say, but couldn't.

Finally the Princess said, "So, let's continue on to the castle. How long until we arrive?"

"I… I cannot be sure. Two days. Perhaps three?" he offered.

"What?" Nilou was completely surprised.

"Well, we will find shelter for tonight. And then a

day's journey down the river before we can cross…"

"Where? We're going to sleep… outside?" She was having trouble breathing.

"I will find us shelter, your Highness."

"We're going to be in the woods? In the dark? Oh my goodness! Oh my goodness!" She collapsed back on the boulder and hugged herself, rocking, repeating, "I hate the rain. I hate it, hate it, hate it!"

"I don't understand," Anoush said. "You should dance in the rain."

"What? What? We were almost killed!"

"Yes, we were almost killed," he repeated, sounding happy about it. "But we were not. We should rejoice."

The Princess stared at the stable boy. She was seriously worried about him. "Are you insane?"

"I'm sorry, I don't… What does this mean?" he asked.

"Are you nuts? Crazy?"

Anoush shook his head, not understanding. "I don't know these words."

"You don't know what crazy means?" she asked, in disbelief. "That, right there, is crazy."

"I am sorry," Anoush said innocently. "Does it mean, "happy"?"

"No!" Nilou said, "It doesn't mean that at all. Oh, my goodness." She was worried that her rescuer was a complete idiot. She sat him down on the rock next to her, and spoke to him as though he was a child: "Insane or crazy is when – and I didn't mean this seriously when I said it to you, not really – it's when someone is not right in the head."

"Not right?"

She nodded, thinking he was understanding now.

"Who decides what is right?" he asked.

"What? Everyone." He obviously wasn't getting it. "Look, everyone thinks a certain way. So if one person thinks totally different than everybody else it means they might be crazy."

"So... it means you are a great thinker," Anoush volunteered.

"No, look, wait," Nilou said, trying one more time, "Here is how it is explained sometimes: If you continue to do the same thing and expect different results, that's insanity."

"Oh..." he said, nodding because he finally understood.

The Princess relaxed, proud that she got through to him at last.

"...It means you are strong of spirit and mind," he said.

"Yes. No. What? Wait? What?"

"It is clear now. If I wanted to break this rock we are sitting on with a large hammer and everyone thinks I cannot do it but I think I can, that is insane, yes? And if I hit it again and again and again and it does not break but I keep expecting it to, that is insane, yes? So when I do finally split the boulder in two everyone says, what a totally insane man he is!" Anoush stood up, proud and smiling.

"Yes," she told him, "you are definitely a crazy man."

"Thank you, Princess."

Princess Niloufar nodded her head to re-assure the crazy stable boy.

He picked up the muddy box, saying, "We should go. We must find shelter before it gets dark."

"Yes, that would be wonderful," the Princess said, mostly to herself. "Because we don't want to wander around the forest, soaking wet, barefoot, muddy, with a crazy man who wants to dance in the rain, and wild animals, in the dark, who want to eat us…" She walked on, wondering if this day could get any worse. "Probably," she thought.

*****

Amazingly – to the Princess, anyway – Anoush located a shallow cave near a sparkling brook. There was an overhang that had protected the area from the heavy rains so the wood was dry and he easily built a fire, then cleared the cave of any brush and insects. Had it been anyone else but Nilou the setting would have seemed beautiful: the golden light of the sun setting over hills, a warm fire with a freshly caught rabbit roasting on a spit. The stable boy knew how to survive quite well in the wilderness.

Nilou sat by the clear water, hidden by a tree, in her undergarments, angrily rinsing the mud from her dress. She looked closer at the dress: beneath the mud there were red stains in several places. "Oh, my goodness," she thought. "I'm bleeding." She figured out where the stains on the dress would be on her body and searched but couldn't find any cuts on her bronze skin.

She looked around to find Anoush so she could ask him what had happened. She spotted him downstream. He was washing his feet and hands in the stream. His feet were cut and bloody from his fall down the ravine, his fingernails were ripped off in places and his hands were a mess. He had been bleeding since he rescued her… but said nothing.

He turned and saw her looking at him and smiled. She was about to smile back when it hit her. She immediately looked away. She covered her mouth with her hand.

"Oh, my goodness." She had no veil! No man should see anything but her eyes and her eyes should give nothing away — that is what she was taught. He could be killed just for looking at her face.

"Are you alright, Princess?" he called to her.

"I have no veil. You should not see my face!" she yelled back.

She could hear his footsteps rustling through the leaves, coming closer. "You must stay back! That is an order!" she said without turning her head. The steps kept coming. "I am warning you, stable boy!" The noise stopped. Then his hand appeared from behind the tree. And in it was her veil: washed and now dry; perfectly matching her dress.

It was the first beautiful thing she had seen since her rescue. She couldn't help the tears from falling. "Thank you, thank you," she cried, taking the delicate piece of silk and holding it to her face.

Her last, "Thank you," was just a breath but Anoush heard it just the same.

*****

Anoush had cooked the rabbit, broke it up into pieces and laid them out on large leaves along with berries he'd gathered for the Princess. He thought he had done everything he could think of to get ready for her but he wasn't prepared at all.

She stepped into the firelight from out of the darkness but to Anoush it seemed as though she had stepped out of a dream. There are so many beautiful things in the world but on this day, at this time, there was nothing more lovely. She had found a way to wash and bathe, decorate her hair with wildflowers; her veil and dress were perfectly matched and flowing in the evening breeze. Now he understood what was in the box he rescued because she was draped in gold and there were jewels in her hair, neck, arms, hands and dainty feet.

Very few people are given the gift of witnessing such beauty. Fewer still would ever know acts of such humble kindness that she bestowed on him next: without a word Nilou knelt beside him and picked up the blade that he had used to carve the food. She expertly slit pieces of her silken dress, making strips of material.

Anoush watched in awe as she skillfully cleaned and then bandaged his feet with the silk cloth… and then she took his hand in hers, cleaned and wrapped his wounds, then did the same with the other hand.

He'd never seen such delicate work, such confidence and care. Whatever this young girl did, she did it perfectly.

*****

They were following the river. Ahead was a village. They'd be there within an hour. Nilou was still piecing together the events of the night before: after bandaging his hands and feet she ate badly cooked rabbit and not-ripe berries without complaint. She was so tired she fell asleep on the cold stone of the cave – no pillows, no blankets – and awoke with the stable boy's garment draped over her.

"Do you think the rest of the caravan will be in the village?" Nilou asked.

"No, your Highness. They are on the other side of the river."

"Oh... Will there be an envoy to escort me to the castle in the village then, do you think?" Nilou asked.

"No, your Highness."

"Okay. Then exactly how are we getting back?" she asked.

Anoush stopped and turned to look at the Princess. "We must trade your jewels for a horse and supplies and make the journey ourselves."

Nilou was in such shock she couldn't even get the words out. Her mouth just kept opening with no sound.

"Not all of them. Just one piece of gold perhaps," Anoush said, hoping to make her feel better.

The Princess was actually shaking she was so upset. "My jewelry? Are you kidding me?"

"What does this mean, 'kidding'?"

"Oh, my goodness," Nilou screamed, "why don't you understand anything that I'm saying?!"

"I apologize, your Highness. Perhaps these are words for the wealthy?" he suggested.

"Oh," Nilou said, realizing she might have insulted the young man. "Umm, kidding means 'fooling'."

"You think I'm a fool?"

"No. I didn't... It's... It's like a joke. Joking?" she explained.

"Ah," he said, finally getting it. Then frowning. "Why would I make a joke?"

"I don't know!" the Princess shrieked, and started crying. She sank to the ground, sobbing, clutching her jewelry box to her chest.

Anoush didn't know what to do to comfort her.

Still weeping, Nilou opened the box and sifted through the perfectly arranged necklaces, earrings, bracelets and rings. She finally held up a lovely, gold and ruby necklace - closing her eyes, not able to watch Anoush take it from her hand.

She didn't look up until she heard the sound of rocks banging into each other.

"Oh, my goodness. What are you doing? You're destroying it!" the Princess screamed.

Anoush stopped banging on the necklace with a rock. "I must take the stones out to sell the gold. No village merchant could afford to pay for such a valuable necklace. And it would draw too much attention."

"I've had that from when I was six years old! It was perfection," she said as though she was mourning the loss of good friend. She let her body go limp to the ground. "Just kill me now," she moaned.

"I'm sorry, your Highness."

The Princess was inconsolable. She walked with her head down, all the way to town, where the stable boy used the gold from the necklace to get them some food, clothing and a horse.

She hardly complained about how incredibly ugly the shoes and robes were.

"We wish to go unnoticed on the road, Princess," Anoush explained.

"You realize that this is exactly the opposite of how I've lived my entire life, don't you?"

So she rode along in an ugly dress with ugly shoes on an ugly horse. At one point an ugly dog started following them. "Perfect," Nilou said to no one in particular.

When Anoush gave the dog some of their food she reprimanded him for it. "You only give dogs table scraps!" she told him.

"Not if you want them to be your friend," he explained.

"Why would you want an ugly friend?" she asked.

"Ugly friends are the best," he told her. "They are more loyal because they know you love them for who they are, not for how they look. They appreciate small kindnesses and find beauty where we may not."

"Fine. Whatever," she said under her breath.

They found a shallow place to cross the river and headed for the main road back home. Before it got dark Anoush found them some shelter, built a fire and brought out the meats, bread and cheese he'd purchased. Nilou washed herself in a cool stream and joined him by the fire.

She lined up the food on the plate they'd bought and made sure that none of it was touching.

"Why do you do that, Princess, with your food?" Anoush asked.

"I think it's beautiful," she said still arranging it. "I know it upsets people and they think I'm foolish or strange but I find such loveliness and comfort in having things in their place. To me, it's like a tapestry of all the things in life: you gather them up, each with its own separate colors and organize them and weave them together - they make a cloth that is so much more beautiful as a whole than each individual part was by itself… because you… organized them." She removed her veil to get ready to eat. "I guess I look at life differently than everyone else."

They sat for a moment by the firelight, thinking.

"So then, you are crazy," Anoush said.

"Yes," she said and smiled at him. "I suppose I am."

Suddenly Anoush understood why women should always cover their faces… because one smile from them could change a man's heart forever.

*****

They reached the main road by midday, talking all the way. Anoush told the Princess how he loved to care for the Royal horses the most: they were such strong and graceful animals. He thought of them as his brothers and sisters – since he had never had any - and treated them with the same kind of care. He was proud of them and proud of his place in life.

"You are proud?" she asked him.

"Oh yes. My people from the north say, 'Be humble for you come from dust, Be proud because you come from stars.'"

The Princess told him about what it's like to have real brothers and sisters and what a pain they can be: jealous and mean and unforgiving, but also how warm they are sometimes: like when she got terribly ill and they all stayed in her room with her, keeping things organized, feeding her and playing games until she was well.

The two were talking so much that they didn't notice the Old Man coming toward them from the other direction on foot. When he got close, he pulled out a large knife and held it to the Princess's stomach.

"Get down off of the horse. It's mine now, along with

everything else. What's in the box?" he asked, referring the Princesses jewelry box.

"No, please don't take this," she begged.

"Get down!" he yelled at them.

Just then the dog snarled and bit the Old Man on the leg. He screamed and dropped the knife.

Anoush kicked the horse and they took off down the road. They looked back to see the dog dragging the Old Man to the ground, snarling and biting, the Old Man trying to defend himself.

Anoush stopped and whistled for the dog, who then let go of the robber and ran toward them.

When the dog caught up to them, Nilou looked down at the ugly mutt and said, "Good dog." And he wagged his tail as if he understood.

*****

By late afternoon they were on the outskirts of the city, with the castle looming ahead.

That's when it started to rain.

"Really?" Princess Nilou said to the sky.

"Are you kidding me?" Anoush yelled up at the rain, laughing. He hopped off the back of the horse and kept screaming at the sky, "You threw her off of a mountain and buried her in earth and you could not stop her! You made her sleep on a stone bed and you could not bruise her! You made her sacrifice her treasure and replaced it with ugly shoes and you did not break her spirit! You sent a robber to steal from her and he could not get a thing! Are you kidding me? Rain? Your rain barely touches this Princess!"

The Princess laughed out loud as she, too, jumped from the horse and yelled to the heavens, "Are you kidding me? Rain? That's all you got? Ha! I laugh at your rain! Haha!"

And she laughed in the rain and jumped in the puddles and danced with the stable boy until they were tired and happy.

As they rode through the city, the Princess's shoulders slumped down. Anoush turned her face toward his to see what was wrong. He couldn't tell if her cheeks were spotted with raindrops or teardrops.

"What is it, Princess?" he asked.

"The last time it rained… a soldier died trying to save my life. How can I ever repay his sacrifice?" she asked.

"By living a life worth saving, your Highness," he told her.

She nodded and was grateful for the tears that fell.

*****

Most of the castle gathered in the great hall to greet the Princess and the stable boy when they returned. Hugs and kisses and tears of joy from the Princes and Princesses, the servants and nursemaids.

The crowd parted as the King and Queen joined them. They were at once deeply grateful to have their daughter back and shocked at her appearance.

"I know I may not look like a Princess, father," Nilou said as she curtsied, "but this man has made me feel like one. He has saved my life in more ways than I can tell you."

With that the King and Queen took their girl into their arms and kissed and hugged her and cried over her, then immediately got her some new clothing.

They repaid Anoush with a job as head of the Royal Stables and moved him into the castle.

The Princess still kept her life fairly organized but you can't really have things too perfect when an ugly dog sleeps on your bed with you and drags in who-knows-what.

Princess Niloufar and Anoush remained friends for life. And they never missed a chance to dance in the rain... of course she'd change right after into something very stylish and neat.

THE END

THE
PRINCES & PRINCESSES
OF TEXAS CHILDREN'S
HOSPITAL

Brinly Pirtle

Brinly Pirtle is 7 and a-half-years old and lives in Texas. She was diagnosed with leukemia (ALL) in 2010 when she was 3 and-a-half years old and went through over 2 years of treatment at TCCC. She is now in the second grade, loves animals and crafts/drawing, and plays softball.

Alejandro Araque

I was born in Brigham and Women's Hospital in Boston, Massachusetts on the 12th of November, 2001; but my dad is from Colombia and my mom is from Puerto Rico. I only lived in Cambridge, Massachusetts for half a year before we moved to Sugar Land, Texas. Sugar Land is just South-West of Houston, Texas. I went to school at The Campbell Elementary School in Greatwood, Sugar Land, Texas. My sister (now aged 8, named Lorena) was born in 2006. My other sister (now aged 5, named Camila) was born in 2009. After living 8 and a half years in Sugar Land, we moved to Norway in 2010 and I went to BISS (British International School of Stavanger). We lived in Norway 3 and a half years and now we moved to Cambridge, England.

I like to read a lot as well as play video games. I love the Harry Potter books and the Hunger Games books. I really love to learn new things and I usually ask my dad so he can explain it to me. One of the things I have enjoyed the most was learning about how an engine works. My favorite subjects are math and science. There is nothing better to eat than pizza. I dislike writing long things, kind of like this biography. My family loves to travel everywhere. We have been to tons of different countries. For example, we have been to Iceland, Spain, Colombia, Italy, Germany and France. I would love to travel to Hawaii.

Brooke Hester

Brooke who just turned 7, doesn't really know a life before her illness. She was diagnosed at age three with Neuroblastoma - a cancer that develops from immature nerve cells found in several areas of the body. Throughout countless treatments and operations, Brooke somehow remains one of the most optimistic, happy children that you will ever meet; she is the cheerleader of the family. After Brooke designed her own "blossom" headband, she noticed other children with hair loss could benefit from one so she and her mother started the foundation, Brooke's Blossom N Buddies. Their mission is two-fold: helping children with cancer directly by providing them hand crafted headwear and raising awareness for the serious need to both find and fund cures for pediatric cancer.

Currently Brooke is recovering from a barrage of stem cell injections and preparing for a revolutionary new trial involving genetically modified T-Cells at the Texas Children's Hospital.

Alekzy Alana Rodriquez

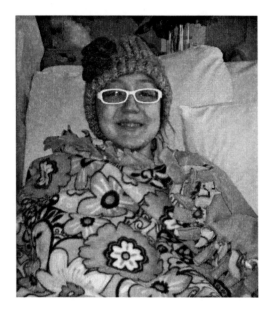

Alekzy Alana Rodriguez was born 1/24/2001. She has always been a very happy person, pleasant to be around. She has 2 brothers and 1 sister. Lekzy was diagnosed with Acute Lymphoblastic Leukemia in March of 2014. She has been hospitalized at Texas Children's since April 2014 undergoing treatment for her very aggressive disease. Lekzy always remains positive and has been inspired to become an RN. She wants to help kids with cancer. She feels that her experience will allow her to relate to them because she will know exactly what they are going through. In her free time Lekzy has always been crafty. She loves to draw, make duct tape wallets, and sing. Her idea for The Princess Who is Very, Very Organized comes from her own lifestyle. She has bags and boxes with everything labeled.

Marc Clark

$\mathcal{THANK YOUS}$

I would like to thank the children and families of the Texas Children's Hospital and Vannie E. Cook Jr. Children's Cancer and Hematology Clinic for inspiring this book.

I'd like to thank Connor, Mrs. Yonemura's Fourth Grade Class at Hesby Oaks Leadership Charter in Encino, California & Ms. Bronson's Third Grade Class at the Balboa Magnet School in Northridge, California for their help.

Special thanks to those who volunteered their talents to help create The Royal Fables: my editor, Marian Grudko, Bryan Clark, the Princess Fables staff and especially Alana Seal whose tireless efforts brought this book into being, and who works and sacrifices every day to bring awareness for the need for more pediatric cancer research to the public and a little joy to the lives of the families struggling with it.

.

ABOUT THE AUTHOR

Marc Clark is the award-winning author of The Princess Fables. The book has been awarded a total of eight writing and illustrating awards including Best Children's Book at The 2014 Beach Book Festival. The book has been in the top 100 Kindle Store for children's ebooks for most of 2014. The paperback edition has hit the number one spot on Amazon's Best Seller List eight times this year.

Mr. Clark currently resides in Manhattan. He is an award-winning author and writer/producer of over 2,000 commercials and television content as well as the HBO Family Series, "30 X 30 Kids Flicks."

Marc Clark